THE POWER
OF STARS

THE POWER
OF STARS

· · · · · · · ·

Louise Lawrence

Collins

To David Elliot

William Collins Sons & Co Ltd
London · Glasgow · Sydney · Auckland
Toronto · Johannesburg
First published 1972
This edition 1989
© Louise Lawrence 1972
A CIP catalogue record for this book is available
from the British Library.

ISBN 0 00 184685–X

I

MISS COTTEREL was leaning from the window brushing breadcrumbs from the board when the five-fifteen bus from Hasley pulled in at the bottom of the path opposite the public house at Green Bottom. She watched for a moment as the three young people with their books and satchels stepped down, black silhouettes against the brilliant light, then closed the window.

She went through to the living-room at the back, littered with books, scientific journals, and piles of papers covered with tiny cramped writing. She didn't put the light on, just groped for the packet of cigarettes she knew were on the table, lit one and went out on to the terrace. She could hear the refrigerator in the kitchen making a low humming noise, the sound of dogs' paws rattling in the hallway and the bus going hollow under the railway bridge.

It was mild for November, but there was a sharpness in the air which smelled of frost. It was not as dark as she had thought. She could make out the shapes of the trees and see a boy going along the lower path. A boy? She *thought* it was a boy. These days it was difficult to tell the difference. He waited for a while, standing still on the path where the light from her kitchen fell across as a strip of yellow. She recognised him. The Keir boy. Someone was running down the road, quick echoing footsteps. The girl? Or the other boy? Whoever it was, Jimmy Keir was waiting for them. She could see the quarries rearing black above the house and the red sky hanging over them. Footsteps came running back up the road. A sheep bleated somewhere. Still the boy waited.

A stone rattled on the other path and he walked on. The emptiness was lonely.

She thought of Leonard's thesis lying unfinished in the laboratory. She'd stay and finish it, then she'd move; somewhere where there were more people. It hadn't been so bad when Leonard was alive. She hadn't even noticed. But she did now. It was lonely.

Impatiently she crushed her cigarette with her shoe. One thing she had never been was sentimental. It must be the atmosphere; the brooding hills and sheer quarry faces hanging over her. The cry of a melancholy owl out hunting. The eeriness of the half-light which made hills and rocks take on supernatural shapes. Her thoughts made her angry. They were the ghoulish imaginings of a child. She was not a child. She was a middle-aged spinster with a calm and logical mind. She looked up.

The stars were hanging in the sky. Piercing. Pouring down their light. Their magnetic brilliance caught her eyes and she stared at them. The accumulation of every ray of cosmic light would create a force greater than the gravitational pull of the sun. The utilisation of that force would produce energy, substantiate a power undreamt of. Ridiculous! The cosmic power of stars was nothing whatever to do with Leonard's thesis on the hypersensitive hearing of bats. She ought to be working on that thesis now. Miss Cotterel dragged her eyes down.

She heard a scream beyond the garden. A scream from the heart of the dark pitted hills. An animal in pain. She saw a flash of light. Harsh blue-white light from the depths of the quarry. Lightning? She knew she had seen no clouds. There had been nothing to break the sharpness of the stars. Miss Cotterel looked up and frowned. Something had changed. The stars . . . they weren't piercing any more. All their power had been drained in a flash of light. Come to earth somewhere

6

nearby. Come to earth in a scream of pain.

She shivered. There would be a frost by morning. The sunset light gleamed on her spectacles. She whistled softly. Her voice was deep and mannish.

'Winston! Randolph! Walkies!'

A hot, strong smell came drifting down from the hills.

'I've got to go to the post,' Jane said.

Alan clung to the seats and swayed down the gangway after Jimmy.

'I meant to go in the lunch hour,' Jane said, 'but I forgot. I shall have to post it now. It's about Gran's pension.'

The bus slowed down suddenly. Jane lurched forward and clutched Alan's blazer. Jimmy stepped down and scowled back at them. Alan followed him into the cold semi-darkness where half-naked trees and grotesque hills reared up to the sky.

'Shall I come with you?' Alan offered.

'No. The post box is only just down the road.'

'Then I'll walk slowly. You can catch me up.'

Jimmy slouched up the path which led through the quarries. His hands were in his pockets and his head was bent to the ground. Alan went after him, stopped and looked back to where Jane was standing on the edge of the road.

'Go on then,' Alan said. 'I'll go slowly.'

She turned and started running. She was a strange girl. Quiet. He heard the echoing rumble of the bus going under the bridge and on towards Langdon. Then the silence came slipping back; dark, profound, engulfing him. He stopped walking. Out of the silence small sounds came loudly. Feet rattling stones. Jane running down the road. A sheep bleating out on the hills. Leaves rustling. Small things going through dry grasses. The air was sharp and smelled of frost.

The first shock of darkness had worn off. He could distinguish shapes, weird and distorted. Black nightmarish shapes he knew were only rocks and bracken. He trod carefully between the stones, keeping Jimmy a few yards ahead. What was biting Jimmy tonight? Alan stopped. Jimmy had turned off the path. Taken the other fork above the bungalow. Where did it go? Round the bottom of the quarries? Alan shrugged, scrunched over the leaves fallen from the oak tree and took the usual path. Something was certainly making Jimmy unsociable. He heard Jane running back up the road.

Walk slowly. She'll catch up.

This place! Even now he wasn't sure of the way, not once he reached the top. Maybe he should have followed Jimmy. What if Jane went that way too? He'd be left to find his own way home. He might lose himself. End up in the woods; fall over a quarry, or down a mine shaft. Four times he'd walked this path. Every evening this week coming home from school. It curved when he wasn't expecting it and the hills rushed around him, shutting him in.

There were hills on either side and ahead. Beyond them rose the quarry face topped by almost leafless trees, black outlines against a flaming red sky. Shepherd's delight. Impressive! Sort of thing Mum would like. He'd have to bring her down this path if he could find it from the other end. It was narrow now. Carved between hills. A gorge. Small paths led off and upwards, winding among rocks and bracken. Sheep paths. Nice to explore on a hot sunny day. Nice and remote. No tourists.

Give me Kew Gardens any day. How can Mum like living here?

The path led into the open, right across the top of the quarry. It was like steps. A gigantic stairway leading up

8

and down. One quarry up behind, one down in front. High and sheer both of them. And down below there were more quarries, more slag heaps. Hills and precipices until you hit the road and went up again; more quarries, more hills, and woods stretching across the top of them. Alan stared at the black landscape. Fabulous view Jane had said, only it was always too dark to see it.

Walk carefully. Trip over a stone and you'll be over that edge. Time to scream before you hit the bottom. Come on, Jane. I can't go much slower. It's cold standing here. Catch me up. I want to talk to you. Jimmy's gone the other way. We'll be able to talk.

He waited in the mixture of sunset and moonrise. Sunset over the quarry behind, moonrise over the woods and the opposite hills. The lights of Hasley were fallen like stars in the valley. Everything was very still. Lonely.

Alan looked up. The stars were shining. Billions of stars. Every one a sun with planets. The light he saw now had left them aeons of years ago. It had travelled across the vast outer reaches of space. The distance was so vast it was incomprehensible. Minute precision of balance. Who'd thought it all out? Who's put them up there? Who'd worked out all the orbits, the revolutions, the gravitational pull of each sun upon each planet in its own allotted sphere? All those circles in the sky. Who had a mind great enough to understand even a tiny portion of a tiny galaxy and control it? Who had a power great enough to control the power of the stars?

If he had all night he could count them. One, two, three . . . seven in the plough. Orion . . . one, two, three. Andromeda . . . one, two, three. Not all night. It would take a lifetime. Their sharp brilliance hurt his eyes. All that light, all that power, coming down from the stars, being concentrated in one place, here where he stood, here on his eyes. The immensity awed him. There was

9

no cloud anywhere to break the power. It was like a humming, moving fast, coming down from the stars. He could almost make it a tune, if he could catch it, hold it.

That was stupid. How could stars sing? But power could sing. Electric power, engines, machines, computers, telephone wires. All different pitches of humming, like a symphony orchestra made of electrical impulses; building to a crescendo of power; waiting to burst right above him. Something was hanging over him using the power of the stars.

He heard someone coming up the path. Not Jimmy. He had gone the other way. These were slow, soft footsteps hardly disturbing the stones. Jane? He waited where she would see him on the lighter part of the path. He waited until he could hear breathing, then he turned round.

Jimmy stuck his hands in his pockets and slouched up the path. Someone ought to be there. Someone personal to shout: come on Jimmy! He should have asked Caroline. She'd have come. Jane wasn't worth bothering with anyway. He couldn't imagine Jane standing on the side line shouting 'come on Jimmy'. She'd stand and watch perhaps, but she wouldn't shout. She ought to be glad to come. No one else ever asked her out. She wasn't very pretty. She wasn't very lively either. Stick-in--the-mud Bates, that was Jane. She'd be sorry on Monday if Lydcroft won three nil and he'd scored them all.

He took the lower path round the bottom of Elgin. Blow Jane! She could go home on her own. She'd change her mind, he was sure of that. She'd come to the match tomorrow. She always did what he wanted. She'd come running and catch him up. He'd take her to Hasley afterwards, to the pictures or something. He listened. Heard Alan going up the top path, a sheep bleating somewhere, someone running down the road. Surely Jane wasn't going home round the road? She couldn't be. She was going down, not up. To the post maybe? He waited. The silence was cold and lonely. Jane came running back. Which path would she take?

She'd see him here waiting. It was light enough for her to see him: moonrise coming up behind Langdon Woods, sunset going down over Winnard's Leap, and the light from the Battery House flooding across the path. Which way would she go? The same way as him? They'd always gone home together ever since she'd been in the first form and he'd been in the third. Of course she'd come this way. She wouldn't choose to go with Alan rather than with him. Jane wasn't like that.

He heard someone walking along the path. Just feet knocking the stones. Good old Brainy Bates! Unless it was a sheep. He'd heard a sheep bleating. Jimmy resisted the impulse to turn round. He crushed a frond of dried bracken in his hand. Which way would she go?

The trouble with Alan was that he was too good-looking and too damned clever. Dark hair, dark eyes, and tall. Ten 'O' levels. Sure to get three 'A's. The Cobbler had welcomed him with open arms to Hasley Comprehensive. Spoke proper, too. Not cockney, even though he had come from London. Sort of refined. No country burr like Jimmy had.

Why did they want to come down here? Must be mad. Why would anyone want to live in a dump like Lydcroft, even if they *had* spent a couple of thousand doing up Amberley House. Show! That's what it was. Country cottage. How quaint. They were a stuck-up lot from London with their landscaped garden, flipping piano, blue saloon and white Triumph sports. That was a sore point. His Mam had said it was Alan's. Mam was usually right. Alan, not eighteen yet, with a white

Triumph sports. Someone had more money than sense. It wasn't fair. All he had was a rotten push-bike.

Why had they moved to Lydcroft? There wasn't anything at Lydcroft. No shops, no cinemas, no dance halls, no coffee bars. Trees, that's what there was. And the chapel, and the football pavilion, and the shop in old mother Morgan's front room. Not even a pub. Just trees, nothing but trees. He could see them now, stark against the sky on top of Winnard's Leap. There weren't even any girls. But birds, yes. Great place for birds was Lydcroft. Tits, woodpeckers, sparrows, cuckoos, the lot!

Jimmy kicked savagely at a stone. She wasn't coming. She must have gone the other way. If she'd come after him he'd have heard her by now, and he couldn't hear anything, just the cold clear silence. Lonely silence. Less than nine more months of mechanical engineering and he was off. London, Liverpool, Bristol, Birmingham, who cared where? There was Elgin towering sheer and black, and Winnard's Leap above it. Old man Winnard had jumped over there. Now Jimmy knew why. Anything to get away from here, from the silence.

An owl hooted. Eerie! A stone fell on the other path. Jimmy looked up. All those silent stars up there, piercingly bright, compelling him to look. All those pin-points of light . . . lump them all together and you'd have something so big it would burn up the earth in less than half a second. You ought to be able to utilise starlight to produce energy. Economical source of power. Terrific power, silent as electricity, a high velocity current passing through the outer limits of the universe. Building up like water behind a dam until it had to burst. If he thought that one out he'd make a fortune. But it was there, all around him, hanging over him, star power.

The owl hooted again. It gave Jimmy the creeps.

There was a scream: harsh, piercing, rising from the

darkness. Jimmy jumped. His heart pounded and the hairs prickled on the back of his neck.

Phew! Don't do that. Gave me the screaming hab-dabs. Rabbit caught in a trap. Old man Bowery's been setting traps again, the cruel old buzzard. One day the warden'll nobble him. Just a bunny. Don't be scared, Jimmy boy. Don't be scared.

He thought something flashed. Blue lightning in Elgin. He stopped where the path branched off. Up there it was, in Elgin, a rabbit in a trap. Maybe he'd go and find it.

In this light? Never! It'd be in the bracken some-where. Poor little codger.

Silence. He'd never heard silence like it. But it was a different silence now. Not sharp any more. And the stars were paler. Not so piercing. Like a fuse blown. Where had it gone? All that power, where had it gone? Blown up in a flash of light in the depths of the quarry, and a rabbit screaming in pain? The heat that came drifting was burning, sharp and strong. The welding together of metals, the fusion of atoms; power, white-hot power drifting from Elgin. Jimmy ran. All right, so he was scared. He'd admit it. Of what he didn't know, but it was something back there too awful to even think of, too powerful to approach. Over the sound of his footsteps rattling the stones he heard someone shouting on the other path.

Race you to the top, Jane girl! That's it, Janie. You shout, kid. Alan'll save you.

Jane ran down the road to the post box. The windows of the houses clustered in Green Bottom were just squares of yellow light. She heard the bus going up the road, sounding hollow under the railway bridge, leaving the silence behind and her own feet beating the road. She posted the letter to the Ministry of Pensions and ran back. She didn't want to go to the football match. She didn't want to stand there and shout. Everyone would stare at her. Why had Jimmy asked her to go? He never had before. And when she said she didn't want to, why did he have to sulk?

She took the quarry path. If she went she wouldn't shout. It was stupid standing there shouting. But if she went home by the lower path and ran she could be at the top before Alan and Jimmy. That way she wouldn't have to meet Jimmy again. She wouldn't have to go to the match. The stones rattled as she went up. Then she stopped.

The light from Miss Cotterel's bungalow fell across the lower path. Jimmy was standing there. Jane felt trapped. He must be waiting for her. She waited in the darkness until he moved on, then took the top path. She'd go slowly now; wait until he'd gone past the place where the two paths met at the top, then go round by Mrs Morgan's shop and home that way.

She went quietly over the oak leaves, along the path which cut a narrow gorge through the hills. A sheep bleated. Jane jumped. It was a funny kind of light. Jane didn't like being on her own. Things took on different shapes, distorted and unfamiliar. She knew it was only a rock, but it looked like something crouching ready to pounce. Nightmare things walked behind her with stealthy tread and little rustling noises. Jane wanted to run back down the path, round the other way and catch up with Jimmy. Or catch up with Alan. She liked Alan, but Jimmy didn't. She turned over a stone, slowly and deliberately, and let Alan go on.

Jimmy doesn't like Alan. Alan talks about things Jimmy never even thinks of. Jimmy doesn't like it because Alan's clever. He doesn't show off. He's just clever and he's nice. Sometimes Jimmy is very stupid. But if

Alan hadn't come Jimmy would have stayed the same. Things would be the same. Going home together. Talking. Picking strawberries. Throwing stones over Elgin. Talking, easy talk, serious talk, rubbish, but always easy. If Alan hadn't come there would be no antagonism and no tension. Jimmy wouldn't be so snappy. Gran had said ask him to mend the fence. She couldn't ask him now. She didn't want to talk to Jimmy. She didn't want to go to the silly football match.

The sky was red over Winnard's Leap: crimson red with black birch trees etched against it. No one could paint that; not catch the luminous glowing quality, the perfect detail. She couldn't paint it but she wanted to. She wanted to do something just once that people would notice.

Up above the sky was indigo with a myriad of stars, harsh twinkling, like rats' eyes when they caught the light. The same wicked malevolent gleam. They were all looking down on her, all those stars, all those eyes. All looking down on her, all their thoughts directed on her, all their power on her . . . Jane Bates going home.

Jane shivered. They weren't eyes, they were stars. And even if they *were* eyes they couldn't possibly see her. They were millions and millions of miles away. Millions and millions of miles of cold empty space between her and them. They were huge really, huge shining suns, powerful suns radiating light. The light was coming down from those hundreds of suns and shining on her. They were shining on her because she was looking at them. She was directing their light with her eyes and they held her stare. Eyes looking at stars, stars pouring on eyes. Their power would come and destroy her in a flash of light. It was hanging over her; hovering, silent and dangerous. So terrible she couldn't bear it. Jane dragged her eyes down.

The path came into the open. The last of sunlight and the first of moonlight met across the top of Elgin and Alan was standing there. He was waiting. Jane had almost walked into him and not seen him. She could hear his breathing. An owl hooted, mournful and sad. It was too late to go back. Alan turned round.

'Hello Jane.'

'Hello.'

'It's taken you a long time.'

'Yes.'

The owl hooted again, silent winged, somewhere in the night out hunting with gleaming eyes. There was a scream : sudden, piercing, shrill. And a flash of light, like lightning, blue-white from the depths of the quarry. Jane went rigid with fear, listening to the echoes bounding from the cliff face, screaming horror everywhere.

'Alan !' Jane shrieked.

He put his arm round her. She was shaking. So was he. The heat came up in a wave, sharp smelling, burning hot, pouring down their throats and stinging their eyes. Alan felt a crawl of fear. Something was down there, something he'd rather not know about. Something silent and powerful. He gripped Jane's hand.

'Let's go.'

He wanted to run. He didn't know why but he wanted to run. Take to the hills and hide. Run away from the smell of heat, and the scream and the power.

'What was it ?' Jane croaked.

'A rabbit.'

'They don't make noises like that.'

'It was a rabbit. Caught in a trap. A rabbit screams in pain.'

'How do you know ? You've only lived in the country a week.'

'It's a rabbit, Jane. I know, that's all.'

16

Jane stopped.

'Jimmy went by the bottom path,' Jane said. 'That scream. It came from over there. Alan, it wasn't a rabbit. It was Jimmy.'

Jane's fingers were small in his hand. Cold. Clinging to him for some sort of comfort. It had sounded like a rabbit but Jimmy *had* gone that way. What could he say? Go back and face it, the heat and the power, and look for Jimmy? The path went across open ground, across grey grass and into trees.

'It wasn't Jimmy,' Alan said. 'There's Jimmy now. See!'

Jimmy was hurrying home. Jane shivered.

'Come on,' Alan said. 'It's cold.'

Jane looked up. The stars were still shining, pale, silent, and gentle. Not powerful any more.

'It was queer.' Jane said. 'They were like eyes all glowing down. Baleful, horrible eyes. Powerful, and I was underneath.'

'You felt it too? So did I. Not eyes though, just the power.'

They stared up at the stars. Their power had gone, given up in a scream and a flash of light. Burnt in a wave of intense heat. Jane moved her hand in his.

'Will you come out with me tomorrow?' Alan asked.

'I can't. I'm going to the football match with Jimmy.'

The rotter. I bet he's never asked her before.

'That'll be nice.'

'Yes.'

Alan loosed her hand.

'Jimmy's nice,' Alan said gallantly.

'Yes.'

He's a yob.

'I wonder why he went the other way?'

'Jimmy!' Jane shouted. 'Wait for me!'

2

'G o i n g somewhere?' Alan asked.

Jane jumped. He fell into step, two sleepers at a time along the disused railway line.

'I was cold,' Jane said.

'Cold? But it's tropical.'

'Down here it might be. We're out of the wind. It was cold up there.'

'Gaberdines aren't the best things for keeping out the wind,' Alan said.

He glanced at it. It was shabby. Too short in the sleeves and worn threadbare in places. She had screwed back her long brown hair and fastened it with a rubber band. Plain Jane. But she had huge grey eyes. Alan pulled a solitary blackberry off a bush. It was pippy and tasteless.

'Why did you sneak off without a word?'

'I told you. I was cold.'

'If you didn't want to go to the match, why did you go?'

'Jimmy wanted me to.'

'Do you always do what he wants?'

Jane shrugged.

'Do you?' Alan demanded.

'What?'

'Always do what Jimmy wants?'

'Of course not.'

'You *are* a daft girl. Fancy standing in that perishing wind watching a football match you didn't want to see, just to please Jimmy. You don't know the first thing about football, do you? You don't know the difference between the goalpost and the centre-half.'

Jane dragged her hand along a spray of scarlet bramble leaves. They fluttered to the ground and drifted along making small trails in the black dust at the side of the line.

'Well, do you?' Alan asked.

'Oh don't keep on,' Jane said crossly. 'If you must know I hate football. I think it's a stupid game, and the people who watch it are stupid, too. So there!'

The railway curved in a half-circle along a shelf of the hills. The Hasley road dived in a gorge under the bridge. Alan leant over the parapet.

'It's a good drop. Ideal place for throwing stones on cars. Pity I'm not nine. Where are we going?'

'I'm going for a walk,' Jane said. 'You can please yourself. There's another half hour left to play.'

'And Jimmy's surname isn't Greaves,' Alan commented. 'Compared to Chelsea Lydcroft's pretty sick. Can't I come?'

Jane pushed back a tendril of hair which had escaped from the band. 'Please yourself.'

Her feet crushed the cinders. Her school shoes were covered with black dust. Alan wondered if she ever wore anything but school uniform. But she had spirit, though. She wasn't as meek as she appeared.

'Have a peppermint.'

'No, thank you.'

'Please yourself,' Alan mimicked.

Her grey eyes regarded him for a moment, scowling then smiling.

'All right. I will. Thanks.'

The sun was strong on their backs and the world around them was brilliant with autumn colours: golds, reds, oranges and browns. Maybe it wouldn't be so bad living in the country. It was too late now, anyway. He

19

was here. He trod on the wire fence. It creaked and swayed and the post was rickety.

'Is that Green Bottom?' Alan asked.

There was a cluster of houses below.

'Yes. That's where we got off the bus. There's the path going up.'

It cut a grey line through the hills opposite.

'What's that place? A bit ultra-modern for round here, isn't it?'

It was a cedarwood bungalow built beside the lower path just beyond the fork. It was stark and new in a landscaped garden with lawns and terraces and scarlet-leaved trees.

'The Cotterels,' Jane said. 'They had it built about three years ago. He was a scientist. He's dead now though. His sister lives there. She's an old maid and she's fat. They named it El Garda. It's got El Garda on the gate but everyone calls it the Battery House.'

'Why's that? She doesn't keep chickens, does she?'

'No. She keeps bats. In that laboratory place down the end of the garden.'

Alan crunched his peppermint. The hotness stung his eyes.

'The Battery House. How original!'

There was a woman going up the quarry path, a woman and a dog made small by the distance.

'That's her,' Jane said. 'Fanny Cotterel. She told Jimmy off one night for making too much noise going up the path. That's a pug she's got with her. She has two. I think they're lovely. They've pathetic squashed-up faces. Jimmy says she's mad.'

'Oh?'

'Bats,' Jane said. 'Mad. Bats. Get it?'

'I see. A feeble attempt at a joke.'

Jane glanced at him.

'Go on,' Alan said. 'Tell me about the bats.'

'She keeps them in cages,' Jane said. 'And lets them fly round the room at night. If you go past you can see them fluttering in the light. She watches them.'

'Interesting,' Alan murmured. 'Bats. Makes a change from cats. Bats and pugs. Interesting. I'd like to meet her.'

'I wouldn't,' Jane said quickly. 'She looks horrid. All grim and humourless.'

'Grim,' Alan repeated. 'Like Elgin.'

The quarries were like scars on the face of the hill. Great grey cliffs of sheer rock, dark and sunless. Alan turned away and stared at the gold gorse which keeled up behind them to the trees at the top. Larches grew at odd angles and warm sun-washed rocks jutted out.

'Langdon Woods,' Jane said. 'They go for miles all along the top there, almost to Hasley. There's an old forestry lodge built right on the edge of Langdon Point. It's falling down. Just the downstairs window frames left. You can see the river and the power station on the other side. At night you can see the lights reflected in the river, like a fairy castle. It's high above the world, Langdon Point. Makes you feel powerful until you look down and the drop makes you feel sick.'

'Vertigo,' Alan said. 'I don't suffer from that. Do we go back the way we came? I saw some ruins on the other side of the road.'

'They're only rough stone walls,' Jane said. 'Iron works. The sheep use them. They stink. We'll go this way.'

She ducked under the fence and took a narrow path down the side of a small quarry.

'I thought you didn't like heights,' Alan muttered.

'This is low,' Jane said, 'compared with Langdon Point. Besides, I've been this way hundreds of times.'

She jumped from stone to stone, twisted through

gorse and bracken, dodged brambles and nettles with the sure-footedness of a mountain goat. Alan skidded behind, his feet slipping on the sheep-cropped turf that made the path. The small hills hid her and she reappeared further down. He tried to hurry and clutched at the bracken stems to save himself from falling. Jane was waiting for him outside Green Bottom public house.

They went up the quarry path.

'Let's go this way for a change,' Alan suggested.

The lower path went by the cedarwood bungalow and cut a curving semi-circle round the bottom of Elgin to join the other path at the top. They met Jimmy coming down. His long hair fell across his face but did not hide his scowl.

'Hi Jimmy,' Alan said.

'Bates, you were supposed to be at the football match with me.'

'She was cold,' Alan said. 'We went for a walk.'

'You could have told me you were going.'

'You were down the other end of the pitch, man. I didn't want to distract your attention. Who won?'

'They did,' Jimmy said sourly. 'Five three. I got one in the corner of the net two minutes from the whistle and a fat lot of good that did.'

'It saved you losing five two,' Alan pointed out.

'It's Potter's goal-keeping that's the trouble. He let through two he should have stopped. You might have stayed, Bates.'

'Her name's Jane,' Alan said.

'How did you know we'd be here?' Jane asked.

Jimmy ran his hands through his hair and scowled again.

'I saw you sneaking off.'

'But you didn't know where we'd gone. Why did you come down here?'

'I just did.'

'Ah,' Alan said. 'The silent something which draws us together. Some power. We should draw a circle on the ground and drop blood in it. We might be able to call up a demon.'

'There's supposed to be a Satanist cult in Little Barton,' Jimmy said. 'I'll let them know you're interested.'

'Ssh!' Jane said. 'Look!'

'What? A werewolf?'

The shadow of Elgin lay dark across the path. The sun slanted across the top of Winnard's Leap and made the rest of the valley yellow. Here it was dark, almost cold.

'No. Look . . . a rabbit.'

'Where?'

'On the path going into Elgin.'

It was a brown rabbit, sitting on its haunches watching them. Jane started along the path, slowly, noiselessly, over the carpet of grass.

'Come on, come on then. You're very tame.'

'She's getting close,' Alan whispered.

'Come on. Come on then.' Jane's voice was soft and cajoling. She put out a hand. Touched it. Felt the fur of its ears, warm and alive. Watched its whiskers twitching, smiled at it.

'You're beautiful, aren't you? Aren't you beautiful?'

Alan squatted on his heels a few feet away. Jimmy crept closer.

'It's tame,' Alan said.

'A wild one, though,' said Jimmy.

'It's hurt,' Jane said. 'Its leg. Poor little thing. Its leg's all crushed. It must be suffering agonies. Its mouth's bleeding, too. What are we going to do? We can't leave it here.'

The rabbit stumbled a few paces, dragged its leg and sat still again.

23

'It shouldn't be allowed,' Jane said. 'It's wicked. The poor little thing. It can hardly walk.'

'Try picking it up,' Jimmy said. 'I'll take it home for our Kath. She likes messing about with animals. Go on. Pick it up. It'll let you stroke it. A quick grab and you've got it. Go on.'

Jane crossed the path, stooping, hand outstretched, hair slipping from the rubber band and falling forward.

'Come on, rabbit. Don't be scared. No one'll hurt you.'

Warm silk fur under her fingers, small trembling rabbit. It turned suddenly and sank its teeth into her arm. Teeth sank deep and sharp into her arm. She gasped and stood up. The rabbit clung to her, its legs kicking the air. Jimmy ran, caught its ears and landed a sharp chop on the back of its neck. Its teeth dragged out. Its legs kicked once more. Jane, white faced and trembling, saw it go limp.

'You've killed it. You've killed it. It was hurt and you killed it.' The blood trickled from her wrist. Alan pulled out a handkerchief.

'Why did you kill it?'

'Well it bit you, didn't it?' Jimmy said. 'And with a leg like that it wouldn't have lived long anyway.'

'You shouldn't have killed it.' Alan wound the handkerchief round her arm.

'They don't bite like that,' Alan said.

'And it never will, not again,' said Jimmy.

'They don't bite,' Alan said. 'Rabbits don't bite. Not like that. They kick, and scratch, and nip, but they don't bite. Not deliberately bite.'

'That one did,' Jimmy said. 'You saw it. Like a flipping bulldog.' He held it up, limp, still warm, limbs hanging down, red blood around its mouth, Jane's and its own. The fur down its injured leg was shrivelled.

'It's burnt,' Jimmy said. 'But it's just an ordinary

rabbit. A dead ordinary rabbit.'

'But they don't bite.'

'I know they don't.'

'It bit Jane though.'

'So you said. I saw it.'

'Why?' Alan asked.

'Why what?'

'Why did it bite Jane?'

'Don't ask me. You're the brains. I'm not a rabbit psychiatrist. Maybe your demon turned up after all. They like blood, demons do. They live on it. Suck it out of people's veins.'

Jane was gripping her wrist. The blood had already seeped through the handkerchief. Jimmy stared at the quarry face, sheer, towering over him, dark. There was something about this place; something brooding, uncanny. It had an atmosphere of gloom that made his skin crawl with fear, made him remember last night. That flash, that hot smell, that piercing starlight hanging over him. Last night a rabbit had screamed. Caught in a trap. Right here in the quarry. This rabbit? An association of memories made him afraid. He sensed he was near something powerful, holding it in his hand. This rabbit? Jimmy hurled it away. It landed with a thud among the bracken.

'Let's get out of here,' Jimmy said.

'You could have given it to your mother to stew,' Alan said.

'You want to stew it, you stew it,' Jimmy said. 'I'm getting out of here. I don't like it, and Bates needs a doctor.'

'Her name's Jane,' Alan reminded him.

'Aye,' Jimmy said. 'It always was.'

'Why did it bite her?' Alan asked again.

'Oh don't keep on, boyo. It's dead now.'

'And you killed it,' Jane said softly. 'You killed it, Jimmy. You shouldn't have done that.'

They walked into the sun and wind at the top of the path. Looking back, the sun caught the windows of the Battery House and turned them into yellow eyes. In the garden a fat woman was watching them.

3

'F i v e stitches,' Nick said. 'He thought it was a dog.'

'Who did?' Alan inquired.

'The doctor in Casualty.'

'And she's all right?'

'She was quiet. Shocked, I'd say. I took her home. Her grandmother was going to put her straight to bed. Most sensible thing to do really, even though she didn't want to go. She'll feel better after a sleep.'

'What's her mother like?' Alan asked.

'She hasn't got a mother,' Jimmy said. 'There's only Granny Bates. It's up here somewhere, Mr Grant.'

'Lead on, lad. And you'd better call me Nick. Hasn't Alan told you? I'm not Mr Grant.'

'I did hear me Mam saying something about . . .'

Jimmy kicked a stone. Mug! He should have remembered Alan's Mum had married twice.

'Up here,' Jimmy said. 'In the bracken.'

'I thought it was farther that way,' Alan said.

Jimmy shrugged.

'Could be. Can I borrow the torch?' He added 'Sir' as an afterthought.

'Here,' Nick said. 'And I'm not knighted. If you won't call me Nick, call me Dr Mackenzie.'

Alan went nearer the quarry face, where the smooth grass floor dived down again into jagged rocks, old cars, rusty bicycle wheels, mattress springs, tyres, tins and black stagnant water. It was too dark to see properly. He only sensed the high sheer rock face leaning over him.

'It's no good looking there,' Jimmy said. 'We'd have

heard it land in all that junk. I chucked it in the bracken.'

There were little tunnels going off the path, scuttled out by small creatures as they came and went. Bigger ones were used by sheep. Jimmy went up and down them, shining the torch through the browning stems of waist-high bracken.

'It went somewhere by this rock,' Jimmy muttered.

Nick started to move the ferns with his foot.

Alan walked back towards the main path, away from the oppressive overhang of Elgin. He could see the lights of Hasley over the edge. The sky had gone from blue-grey to blue-black and the stars were beginning to appear. He went slowly up a side path, peering at the ground. His foot knocked against something metal. Alan squatted down. It was a foot pump. He examined it. It looked all right. Why had it been thrown away? It was too dark to see. The torch was dancing where Nick and Jimmy were searching and someone was watching him.

Alan looked up. On a level with his own was a pair of unwinking black eyes and a pale squashed face surrounding them.

'Winston!' The pug waddled away. There was a bandage round its front leg, gleaming white in the darkness. A fat woman was standing on the path like a statue of Buddah in the gloom. The two small pugs sat stiffly at her feet. Nick came loudly through the bracken.

'The name's Cotterel,' the woman said. '*Miss* Cotterel. Have you lost something?' Her voice was deep, like a man's.

'As a matter of fact we have,' Nick said. 'A rabbit. I don't suppose you've seen one?'

'Saw one this afternoon. Poor little blighter. Winston fetched it out.'

Alan jumped to the path.

'Was its leg crushed?'

'It was,' Miss Cotterel said. Her thick spectacles glared owlishly at Alan.

'We found it, too,' Alan said. 'Just before tea. It must have been the same one. It had been in a trap.'

'They scratch,' Miss Cotterel said. 'And I wasn't wearing gloves. Went home to fetch some and a box to put it in. It was gone when I got back. Rather peculiar, I thought. The dogs wouldn't have anything to do with it once they'd fetched it out. Its leg was burnt.'

'You noticed,' Alan said. 'Jimmy noticed, too.'

'I did. I was curious. Picked it up and it kicked like the devil. Big rabbit.'

'It didn't bite you?' Nick said.

'Nipped Winston. Didn't give it a chance to nip me. Had it by the ears. Kicked, though. I couldn't hold it. Curious, its leg being burnt.'

'I'm curious too,' Nick said. 'Jimmy killed it. Threw it in the bracken. I was hoping to find it and do a dissection.'

The woman's voice hardened. 'Pity today's youth can't find anything better to do with their time than killing wild life. All this long hair and hooliganism. Ought to be birched.'

'Don't blame Jimmy,' Alan said hotly. 'That rabbit had rabies or something. It bit Jane.'

'Yes. They do nip when they're scared. No reason to kill the beast, though. All you young people live for is violence. Never happier than when you're hurting or maiming something.'

Alan clenched his fist. 'There's people I know who make a great show of condemning cruelty to animals but they still sit down and enjoy their lamb chops and roast chicken. It didn't nip Jane. It deliberately bit her. One minute she was stroking it. Next minute it sunk its teeth in her arm. She's had five stitches. Now don't tell me

29

Jimmy had no reason to kill it.'

'Alan!' Nick said warningly. He turned to the woman. 'I took the lass to hospital myself. The bite was deep enough for them to give her an anti-tetanus injection.'

'Humph!' Miss Cotterel grunted. 'Is that the girl Bates who gets off the Hasley bus?'

'Yes,' Alan said. 'Jane Bates.'

'Usually see you go by,' Miss Cotterel said. 'Saw you last night. Well, let's find this rabbit. Where've you looked?'

Miss Cotterel hitched up her skirt and bull-dozed through the bracken. The pugs waddled behind.

'People like her make my blood boil,' Alan hissed.

'And you were nothing short of insolent,' Nick hissed back. 'Watch it in future.'

'Long hair doesn't make us hooligans.'

'She meant Jimmy, not you.'

'Jimmy isn't either. Look at her . . . charging through there like an old cow through a hayfield. That rabbit'll be mashed to pulp if she steps on it.'

'Alan . . .'

'Well, look at her, the fat old bag.'

'You watch your tongue! I've heard quite enough common abuse for one night.' Nick's soft Scottish accent was angry.

'I don't like being got at by narrow-minded old spinsters. And who are you to tell me what to do? You're not my father. When are you going back to London?'

'Tomorrow night.'

'Good.'

'One day I'll take my belt to you, whether your mother likes it or not.'

The sheer walls hung over them and the stars poured down their light. Piercing.

'This place gives me the willies,' Alan muttered. 'What

the heck do you want to dissect it for? It's only an ordinary rabbit and it's dead.'

Nick was staring up at the stars.

'Not ordinary,' Nick said. 'Ordinary rabbits don't go round biting people.'

There was a shout and Jimmy came charging towards them.

'Good lad!' Nick said.

'I haven't found the rabbit, Dr Mackenzie,' Jimmy said. 'I've found the trap.' He stopped. 'Good evening, Miss Cotterel.'

'Good evening James.'

'Let's see,' Alan said.

Jimmy shone the torch on it.

'Strewth!' It was just a shapeless mass of metal parts welded together. Melted and solidified again.

'That's not a trap, surely?' Nick said.

'It was,' said Jimmy. 'Those were the main springs; there and there. Looks like someone's been to work with an oxyacetylene welder to free a rabbit?'

'Not a welder,' Miss Cotterel said. 'A welder would have killed the rabbit. Slow continual heat would have killed it. This was something quick. Just burnt his leg. Flash of intense heat. Maybe lightning.'

'Lightning would have charred it to a cinder,' Jimmy said scornfully. 'Something like lightning . . .'

He was looking up at the sky, remembering. Seeing the stars high and strong, and remembering. A scream, a flash of light, the smell of heat.

'Never mind, Jimmy,' Nick said. 'Let's leave it. I was curious, that's all. But it's not important.'

Everything was very still, very silent; and the sound of a stone falling came loud. The little pug had fixed his white face towards the high top of the quarries, the line where the rocks met the sky. Alan looked, too. Some-

31

one was standing on top of Winnard's Leap, beyond the black trees, a silhouette against the last paleness of the sky. Someone as high as the stars, alone under their stabbing light, drinking their power.

'They were up there last night,' Alan said.

'What were?' Miss Cotterel asked.

'The stars. Yellow hypnotic eyes. Hard, like they are now.'

'You are observant,' Nick murmured.

'I know what you mean,' Jimmy said. 'I'm going. I'm getting out before something happens.'

In the stillness before movement they watched the figure standing against the sky. It was a girl. They could see the wind moving her hair. They could see the stars growing softer as she drew down their light with her staring eyes. In the absolute silence Alan waited for a scream.

'She didn't go to bed,' Jimmy said.

'Who?' Nick asked.

'Jane,' Jimmy said. 'That's her up there.'

'Don't be daft,' Alan said. 'You can't tell from this distance.'

'That's her,' Jimmy said. 'I know.'

'The Bates girl?' Miss Cotterel asked.

'Aye,' Jimmy said. 'Her name's Jane. That's our Jane, up there with the stars.'

The scream Alan waited for never came.

4

'Y o u can't always blame Potter's goal-keeping,' Alan said. 'Your dribbling's messy. You should have had a shot with that last run through, but you let them take it off you. Keep the ball close to your feet.'

'Aye,' Jimmy muttered as he bent his head to the road. 'It's easy to stand on the side-line telling me what's wrong. Try doing it and it's different.'

'Still, four three is better than five three,' Alan said. 'A couple more weeks and it could be a draw.'

The rain was blowing right in their faces, dripping from their hair. It bounced off the road and gleamed on the blue car parked outside Amberley House. Alan noticed one tyre was flat.

'Nick's back,' Alan said. 'He's got a puncture. He *will* be happy.'

'It's your Mum I was thinking of,' Jimmy said.

'What about her?'

'She's young.'

'Thirty-eight.'

'But she looks young. Pretty too. She's not fat.'

Alan thought of Jimmy's mother. She was fat. Frizzy permed hair and blue curlers. Compared with her Anna looked like Helen of Troy. He swung open the gate and wondered if Jane had come.

The concrete path gleamed with reflected sky. Jimmy blew a drop of rain from the end of his nose and dropped his duffle bag and football boots in the porch. Alan opened the door.

'Smoke!' Alan gasped. 'Nick!' he shouted. 'The kitchen's on fire. Nick!'

Nick's voice came from inside. 'Don't panic. Just leave the door open.'

The kitchen was full of smoke, whirling in blue-grey spirals out through the door, curling up in the rain. The smell was hot and strong.

'Has Mum burnt the chips?'

'No she hasn't.'

'Where are you?'

'Over here.' Alan groped to the stove. Nick was coughing somewhere. He peered in the chip pan.

'These chips are done.'

'Well, put them in the oven then.'

'Where's Mum?'

'Gone upstairs.'

They were moving shadowy shapes within a mist.

'Afternoon, Jimmy,' Nick said. 'How's Lydcroft United?'

'Sloppy,' Alan said.

'Who won?'

'They did,' Jimmy said.

'What happened?' Alan demanded.

The smoke was beginning to clear. Nick was changing the plug on the washing machine. Alan clattered plates into the oven and dropped a fresh handful of chips into the pan. Jimmy was standing by the door holding his dripping anorak.

'Hang it up,' Alan told him. 'These sausages want turning, too.'

'Then turn them. Ouch! This thing's hot.'

'I suppose my clever mother dropped the plug in the tub and then switched on?'

'She said it blew up,' Nick said. He fitted the plug in the socket and switched on. Nothing happened.

'Fused?' Jimmy suggested.

34

'I've changed the fuse and the plug. There's no life at all.'

'Frayed lead?' said Jimmy.

'She said it wasn't the lead or the plug. She said it was the washing machine itself. She came racing into the living-room saying it had blown up. There was a flash.'

'A frayed lead would cause a flash.'

Nick handed him the screwdriver. 'Here you are, Jim. You're the mechanical genius. You find out what's wrong with it.'

Jimmy started his examination. Alan towelled his hair. Nick took over the stove, swishing chips around in the fat.

'It's not the lead,' Jimmy said. 'Must be a short circuit somewhere. I could undo them screws there and take the back off.'

'Carry on.'

The rain was lashing against the window. Nick closed the door.

'Where's Jane?' Alan asked. 'Hasn't she come?'

'She was doing the chips whilst Anna finished the washing. She's probably in the other room or upstairs with your mother. Gave them both a bit of a fright. Jane looked like a ghost. Ashen. I'm afraid your mother was in such a panic I didn't pay much attention to Jane. Damn! The sausages!'

Nick rushed back to the stove. Alan stared at the door which led through to the hall. Jane was here. He wanted to go and talk to her. A screw dropped on the floor and curved in a circle towards him. He bent and picked it up.

'She was there again,' Jimmy said. 'Did you notice?'

'Who?' Alan asked.

'The Bat woman. Under the pavilion.'

'I didn't see her.'

'She wasn't there at the beginning. I saw her at half-time. She was gone before the end.'

'Watching me?'

'The woman might be as mad as a coot,' Jimmy muttered, 'but she's not that daft. I tell you it was Jane she was looking for. When she realised she wasn't coming she went away.'

'Is there some mystery?' Nick asked. 'Can I know?'

'Fanny Cotterel,' Jimmy said. 'She's been keeping an eye on Jane. She's always walking down the path when we go up, coming home from school. She looks right at Jane every time.'

'Is that the large lady we met in the quarry when we were looking for the rabbit?'

'That's the one,' Jimmy said. 'She keeps bats in the laboratory down the bottom of her garden. She's taken to coming to the football matches the last few weeks. Not to watch football, mind you, but to watch our Janie.'

'No wonder Lydcroft always loses,' Alan said. 'You're supposed to watch the ball, not her.'

'Does Jane think she's being watched?' Nick asked.

Jimmy put the last screw on the table and loosened the back of the washing machine.

'If she does, she hasn't said anything,' Alan told him. 'Personally I think it's a bit far-fetched. One of Jimmy's crack-pot theories.'

Jimmy pulled the back away and gave a low whistle. The metal parts inside were fused together, welded by some intense heat into a single mass, still hot, still solidifying, still smelling strong. Nick went behind him.

'The whole motor,' Jimmy said. 'The whole motor's blown up. They could have been killed, both of them, if they'd been touching it.' There was a moment of silence except for the chips frying gently in the pan. In the other room the piano began to play.

'But why?' Nick asked.

'Don't know,' Jimmy said. 'Short circuit somewhere? Shouldn't have done that, though. It's dangerous. Voltage too high perhaps? How could it be? Only an ordinary three-point plug. How could it build up a voltage terrific enough to blow the motor?'

Alan opened the door to the hall. The sound of the piano came louder.

'It's like that trap,' Jimmy said.

'The rabbit trap you mean?' Nick asked.

'Yes. All welded together.'

'Coincidence.'

'Is it? Coincidence is queer. This is too queer. It's not only queer, either. It's something powerful, something dangerous.'

'Steady, Jimmy. That's a bit wild.'

'Is it? That flash Mrs Mackenzie saw. We saw a flash too. We heard a rabbit scream and saw a flash. Like lightning. We could smell the heat even in the open air. Hot and strong. Same as when we came in just now. Maybe Jane knows.'

'Jane's a girl,' Nick said, 'What would she know about the inside of a washing machine?'

'She was here,' Jimmy said.

'Yes,' said Nick. 'She was here. I heard her tell Anna to turn it off. I thought she meant the chips.'

'She could have meant the washing machine. She could know.'

Alan was leaning against the door post listening. The music flowed through him, a strange and beautiful sequence of notes, a composition he had not heard before. Poignant. Moving from gentleness to strength, building towards a crescendo, becoming powerful and yet so utterly sad. Tschaikovsky? Beethoven? Which one? Neither, but a great artist pouring out his soul.

'Who's that playing?' Alan asked.

Nick slammed the back on the washing machine.

'Why in the hell Anna couldn't have turned it off . . .'

'Shut up, Nick,' Alan said. 'Listen to that. Isn't it great?'

Nick looked up.

'Someone's playing my piano,' Alan said. 'Who?'

'Jane of course,' Nick said. 'It's not Anna. The only thing she can play is "Waltzing Matilda".'

Jimmy picked up a screw.

'Brainy Bates? Playing that? Come off it. She doesn't know the difference between a pair of bagpipes and a piccolo. She's about as musical as a tom cat courting.'

'Then it must be a record.'

'Do you think I don't know my own piano when I hear it? I've been playing it ever since I was seven. Nick! Look at the chips!' Blue smoke was whirling up.

'Go and tell your mother my name's not Craddock,' Nick told Alan as he moved the pan. 'What an afternoon! Pouring rain, flat tyre, burnt chips and eighty pounds to buy a new washing machine.'

'And Chopin's funeral dirge in E flat,' Jimmy added.

The sound of rain and voices receded far into the distance. The piano keys were a blurr of black and white. Jane stared at them. They were notes of music. She knew nothing about music. She was so tired. She wanted to close her eyes and drift away, but something was fighting, struggling against the tiredness, making her stare at those black and white notes. Stare at them and stare at them until there was nothing else but the notes on the keyboard. Some were high, some were low. She knew that much.

She sat down on the stool. One finger touched one key. One note of music sounded sharp. And suddenly she knew how to make music. It burst in her mind, sweet and sour, sad and beautiful. It drove her thoughts away and made her hands obey. Music came softly at first, then built up. Jane could feel it inside her building up, building up, a torrent of emotion pouring from her. Not *her* emotion, not *her* music. She only shared the moment of making. She made the music they had dreamt of through an aeon of silence. She played for *them*, not for herself. She played until she heard Alan in the hall. His voice broke their power. Jane stared at the black and white keys. They were notes of music to some people, but she didn't know how.

Alan stood at the bottom of the stairs.

'Mum! The chips are ready for you to dish up. Mum! Nick says his name's not Craddock!' The music stopped suddenly and the piano crashed shut. Alan went into the front room, silent over the carpet. Jane was sitting by the fire. Her fingers were pulling at the hem of her skirt.

'Why didn't you tell me?' Alan asked.

She looked up. Her face was white, drained white, dominated by her huge grey eyes, framed by her straight brown hair.

'Why didn't you tell me you could play like that?' She didn't understand.

'The piano, girl. I was listening. You were brilliant and you never said a word.'

He sat on the arm of the chair. Outside the daylight was dull grey and the rain came against the window with sharp sounds.

'Nick's dishing up,' Jimmy said. 'You've to come and get it.'

'Yes,' Alan said. 'In a minute.'

The piano was closed. There was no music sheet on the stand.

'That music you were playing,' Alan said to Jane. 'What was it called?'

Jane's fingers tore at her skirt.

'I can't play the piano,' Jane said. 'I don't know what you're talking about. Your Mum . . . I told her to turn it off. I told her.'

She went past Jimmy into the kitchen.

'Who's mad?' Alan asked. 'Me? I heard her.'

Jimmy stared after her.

'One of you must be,' Jimmy said. 'Because I'm not. Her. She knows.'

5

C L O U D S hung low over the roofs mixing with smoke
from winter chimneys and dropped a cold drizzle over
Langdon. The streets shone with reflected light. Christmas-
coloured baubles made rainbow spots on the pavements
broken into spectrums which feet destroyed as they
walked across them. Boots gleamed and car wheels sent
up a fine white spray. A drift of hot chips mingling with
raw cold and petrol fumes reminded Jimmy he was
hungry. He glanced at his watch.

'Another quarter of an hour before Nick comes. Let's
have a coffee.' The traffic lights flashed amber, then red.
Jimmy dived across the road into the café on the other
side. The smell of chips gave way to the fragrance of
coffee loud with music from the juke-box.

'Just coffee?' Alan asked.

'And a ham roll,' Jimmy said. 'I'll be at the table by the
window. Give us your bag.' It was a navy-blue travelling
bag with B.O.A.C. written in white letters on the side.
People would think he was off to New York if they didn't
know it was full of Alan's shopping. Jimmy thrust his
own battered duffle bag under the table and wiped away a
circle of steam from the window with his anorak sleeve.
Outside the world went wetly by : Langdon, two Saturdays before Christmas, chaos. Everyone out there thought
it was the hub of the world. They'd probably never
been further afield than Hasley. It was a backwater of
society, that's what it was. One day he was going to New
York for a holiday.

'Thirteen,' Alan said. Jimmy put his hand reluctantly
in his pocket. Thirteen flipping pence for a ham roll and

coffee. Robbery! That's what it was. Alan wouldn't miss thirteen pence. He only had to ask Nick or his mother and they handed over pound notes by the dozen.

'You coming to the match this afternoon?' Jimmy asked. He felt a ten penny piece in his hand and left it there.

'Probably.'

'Mike Jones would put you in.'

'No, thanks.'

'Not want to get your boots dirty?'

'I play at school because I have to,' Alan said. 'Not because I like playing football.'

Jimmy stirred his coffee. Alan had forgotten the thirteen pence. If he didn't like football why did he come and watch? So he could talk to Jane while Jimmy was playing football and couldn't hear what they were saying?

'Is Jane coming?' Alan asked.

'She said she was.'

'She hates football.'

'Jane does?' Jimmy sounded surprised. 'Who said so? Did she?'

'It's obvious. She's bored to tears.'

Jimmy scowled. 'She's not bound to come.' He bit his roll. If she didn't like football why did she come? So she could talk to Alan while Jimmy was playing and couldn't hear what they were saying? He'd thought that already and the thought galled him. He and Jane had been friends long before Alan came around.

'Lydcroft's not exactly League Division One standard,' Alan pointed out. 'There's Nick.' He banged on the window. Nick waved and turned in at the door. He came with a rush of cold air.

'More coffee?'

'No,' Jimmy muttered. Nick bought himself one.

'Are you waiting to go?'

'Aye,' Jimmy said.

'Right. Shan't be a minute. Ugh! This coffee is worse than British Rail. Where's Jane?'

'Still shopping,' Alan said. 'We told her to come here and you'd pick us up at twelve. It's only five to now.'

'We can wait,' Nick said. 'And how is Jane? I didn't see her last week-end.'

'Queer,' Jimmy said.

'Why's that?' Nick asked.

'She's developed a thing about machines.'

'Thing? What thing?'

'Oh,' Alan said. 'I'm with you now. Yesterday in the physics lab. Yes, it was queer, come to think about it.'

'She nearly went berserk,' Jimmy told Nick. 'We've got a new computer in the physics lab. Old Cobbler's pride and joy it is. Croons over it like a baby he does. We took Jane to see it yesterday. She nearly went beserk. Said we didn't need a computer. We had brains. Why didn't we use them? One day we wouldn't be able to. We'd have forgotten how. We wouldn't be able to think at all. Only computers would think, not us. She got in quite a state about it.'

'I've a cousin who's terrified of telephones,' Nick said. 'She can't even bear to be in the same room as one. It's quite a common phobia and Jane gave a reasonable explanation. Logical in a way, even if it is rather far-fetched. Hardly berserk.'

'You weren't there,' Jimmy said. 'You should have seen the way she looked at it. As if she wanted to blast it off the face of the earth. Like she loathed it. And it's not just the computer. She's the same going home on the bus. All tensed up. Just sits stiff and grits her teeth. Right, Alan?'

'I wouldn't know. It's you she sits by. She's always

43

all right walking up the path. Quiet, perhaps.'

'Quiet!' Jimmy said. 'That's the understatement of the year. If the stars are shining you can't get a word out of her. She stares at them all the way home. And that old bag from the Battery House following her about with her beady eyes. Not quiet. Queer. Bloody queer!'

'That phobia about machines could be psychological,' Nick said. 'A psychological reaction to something that happened way back in her childhood, suppressed by her sub-conscious mind. Perhaps a mechanical noise frightened her. She mightn't consciously remember, but the underlying fear is there.'

'Freud?' Alan asked.

'Can't be,' Jimmy said. 'She wasn't like it before.'

'Before what?'

'I dunno.'

'You said she wasn't like it before. You must have been thinking of some specific time or happening.'

'You asked me how she was,' Jimmy said, twiddling his spoon. 'I said she was queer, that's all. It's just my opinion. I wasn't trying to make a case of it. All I'm saying is she's got some bee in her bonnet about going on buses and she never had a bee in her bonnet before.'

'Before what?' Nick demanded. Jimmy looked at Alan.

'Before you came,' Jimmy said. Before Alan came with his white sports car and his high-faluting ideas. Freud, Beethoven, discussions on D. H. Lawrence going up the path. It made Jimmy look like an ignorant yob. Trying to make Jane into something she wasn't. Someone stuck up enough to go to tennis parties and literary discussions and turn up her nose at bingo on Fridays and fish and chips on Saturdays, and football. Jimmy stared through the window. What they didn't realise was that it was Langdon out there, not the flipping West End.

'And how in heaven's name can I be the cause of

Jane's mechanical phobia?' Alan asked.

Jane was on the opposite pavement.

'Look at her,' Jimmy said. 'Now don't try telling me she's not stark raving mad. Just look at her.'

'Who?' Nick asked.

'Brainy Bates. Out through the window. Look at her.'

Through the circle of window Jimmy had wiped clear they could see Jane standing outside the supermarket on the other side of the road. She was standing quite still with her hands over her ears. Her shopping bag had fallen at her feet, tins rolled across the pavement and people went by her like a stream of water broken by a rock. Alan pushed back his chair.

'Stay here,' Nick said. 'I'll go. The car's in the park. You two come when you're ready.' He left his cup of coffee unfinished on the table, a dark brown skin congealing on the top. Alan stared at it. Jane hadn't changed just because he'd come. Jimmy had never bothered to think of her before. He'd never noticed her. She'd always been there. She was just Brainy Bates, a person to drag to the football matches when no one else would come. Jimmy had never really thought of Jane at all.

'That woman!' Jimmy said. 'She must have been following her again. By heck, she's got a huge backside.'

Nick was waiting to cross the road. Miss Cotterel was picking up Jane's shopping. Jane was clutching a small white dog.

'She's going with her,' Jimmy said. 'Jane's going off with the bat-woman. We ought to stop her.'

'Why?' Alan asked. 'Because you don't like her? She might be quite human. At least she stopped and helped.' Jimmy's vivid blue eyes were thoughtful.

'She's been watching Jane,' Jimmy said. 'She's been watching and waiting. Now she's got her what's she going to do?'

45

'You tell me,' Alan said. 'You're the one playing Sherlock Holmes. I don't know.'

'Nor do I,' Jimmy said. 'But there has to be a reason. I bet Jane knows.'

The noise of the traffic vibrated inside Jane's head. Even in the shop she could hear it, whirring, vibrating, roaring, a combination of mechanical sounds merging together, increasing in volume until she thought her head would burst. They didn't need cars. They had legs to walk on.

The adding machine clicked on the counter.

They didn't need that either. They had brains to add up. Human logic. They didn't need machines.

She stared unseeingly at the piles of tins and listened to the noise going round in her head, circles and spirals of noise. The stars whirling in their orbits made no noise, but they were more powerful than machines.

Jane looked up. There were no stars, only the hard orange fluorescent lights which flickered and buzzed. She couldn't stand it any more, the noise all around her, the noise of machines. She had to escape before they engulfed her, swallowed her up and she became part of them, no longer herself but part of a machine, no longer dependent upon her own powers but dependent on the machine. She had to escape before she became just a cell of a mind locked inside them, without a body to free herself, without hands to obey the orders of her brain, without legs to run with. Escape before she became just a cell of a mind which knew but could not communicate because it had no voice, no face, no eyes, no expression and no feeling. Only knowledge trapped inside a machine. Just a nothingness with knowledge, terrible, tragic knowledge. A mind which after millions of years of thinking used the power of stars to escape, used the power of stars to

46

whirl through the empty void of space searching for a body. Not again; she couldn't bear it again, the million million years of being nothing, reduced to nothing by these machines. She had to escape from them before it happened.

She fled from the shop. The assistant stared after her and shrugged.

Outside the drizzle felt cold, wet, like tears coming down. Jane wished she could fly. Go up to the sky where the rain came from. Up, up like a bird, up above the iron grey blanket of clouds to where the stars were bright pools of power against the velvet black space. Use the power of the stars. Everyone would be machines unless she stopped them. But she was not a bird. It was daylight. There were no stars and not enough power, just the machines which swished spray on the road, turning wheels and turning engines. Petrol fumes and noise which made her feel sick.

Jane dropped her shopping bag and put her hands over her ears to shut out the sound. She had never felt so alone. Every day the loneliness grew worse and there wasn't anyone to understand except a little dog, a little white squash-faced dog who knew everything she did.

A rough tongue licked her leg.

'Come on, dear,' a deep voice said. 'I've picked your shopping up. I'll take you back to Lydcroft. You come back with me. I've been wanting to talk to you for a long time. Frightens you, doesn't it? All this noise. All these machines. Frightens Winston, too. He can't tell me but I know just the same. I found that damned rabbit and what was inside it. So I know how you feel, love.'

Jane clutched the dog; small and warm, moving and alive. There was a scar on his leg where the rabbit had bitten him, like the scar on her arm. It made them the same. She felt a rush of love.

47

6

T H E bellringers were practising. Chimes mingled with the tramping of feet, crunching frost and ice on puddles. The lantern light was paled by the brilliance of moonlight. Shadows of trees fell blackly across the path, and they went mottled through moonlight and shadow along the drive to Lydcroft Green Farm, the little pug dog with them. A farm dog started barking, sharp insistent yapping. People were moving inside the house, dancing outlines on the curtains. They stood in a circle ready to sing. It was three days before Christmas.

Silent night, holy night,
All is calm, all is bright . . .

Jane stood on the edge of the circle, feeling the frost coming cold up through her shoes, listening to the voices and the bells. It was like hearing for the first time. Each sound, separately and together, voices and bells, was new and different. Above her hung the stars where there was no sound, only eternal silence.

Seeing was new, too. Her sight was sharpened and intensified. Tiny crystals of frost gleamed on the roofs and the road. There was a stark contrast between light and shadow, between trees which were black and fields which were white. Everything moon-washed. And when a cloud drifted across the moon everything was suddenly dark, breathing was whiter and the circle of lamp-light sharper.

A compulsion made her look up. There were the stars, brilliant without the moon. Piercing. All the clouded nights without them had been like a pain. She'd stared from her bedroom window, wandered around the hills and seen only clouds. But she could see them now, those bright, far-away stars. She could see their light with her eyes. She could draw down their brilliance, a million spots of light converging on her eyes. She could store it away in her mind, the starlight, a reservoir of power.

She was suddenly aware of her body, her hands and feet that could move. Eyes and ears with which to see and hear. She was no longer just knowing and being among the awful silent stars. She had a voice which could sing.

Silent night, holy night,
All is calm, all is bright . . .

She scooped up the pug and held him close. He licked her face. If he had thoughts they would be like hers: happy. She needed nothing else, only herself, and the power of stars now and then.

Fifteen young people walked back into Langdon glowing with sherry and mince-pies. Jane was with them, laughing with them, and the pug waddled behind on its short legs. It was the first time Alan had seen her really laughing. They walked along frosted pavements, past the council houses, down the hill to the square where strings of coloured lights hung across the street and a decorated Christmas tree gleamed by the clocktower.

'How long's she had that dog?' Jimmy asked Alan.

'Since last week.'

'Pedigree pugs cost money. Has Granny Bates won the pools?'

'It's Winston,' Alan said. 'They took to each other, so Miss Cotterel let her keep it.'

'Who told you?'

'Jane did.'

'Funny, our Mam never said.'

'The bat-woman took Jane to Hasley yesterday,' Alan

49

informed him. 'They had lunch in Lewises. She's going to dinner with her on Boxing Day and she bought Jane that new coat.'

'The bat? Bought Jane a new coat?'

'Yes. It suits her, doesn't it?'

Jimmy stared at Jane going past the chemist shop window. The coat was jade green with black fur collar and cuffs. It changed her. Made her hair look honey-brown instead of mousey. She was almost pretty. He'd never seen Jane without her school uniform. Gaberdine or blazer, grey skirt and blouse. She even wore school uniform to chapel on Sundays. That coat changed her.

'Why?' Jimmy asked.

'Why what?'

'Why should that woman buy her a coat? You can't buy coats for ten pence. They cost money. And giving her that dog, taking her to Hasley . . . why?'

'You tell me,' Alan said.

'She doesn't even know Jane.'

'She does now. They're friends.'

'The bat and Jane? Friends?'

'Jane likes her.'

'The bat?'

'Yes. She likes her.'

'It stinks,' Jimmy said. 'She followed her around for weeks. She watched her. Now she gives her the dog. Takes her out. Buys her things. Why? It stinks.'

'And why shouldn't she?' Alan asked. 'I bet Jane's never had a new coat in her life. Seems to me she's not had much of anything. Her gaberdine's two sizes too small. She's been stuck in this godforsaken part of the country with an old woman to look after her all her life. It's time someone did something.'

'There's a reason,' Jimmy said. 'People only do things like that for a reason.'

'Like you drag her to football matches when no one else will go,' Alan remarked.

'Sorry I spoke,' Jimmy muttered and swung into the coffee bar.

Jane was standing by the table clutching the dog. Jimmy noticed her eyes, how big they were. Grey far-away eyes. Dreamy. He'd never noticed them before. It was that coat. It did something for her. Jimmy pulled out a chair.

'Sit down, gorgeous. I'll buy you a coffee.'

Jane started.

'Oh . . . thanks.'

She sat down and put Winston by her feet. He gazed up at her with pathetic eyes.

'Get me one, too,' Alan said.

The air was thick with tobacco smoke. People talked and danced. The coffee machine hissed. Heat steamed the windows and the juke-box screamed music. Jane's hand rested protectingly on Winston's head. She bent and spoke to him.

'Don't worry. We'll go soon. It won't be for long. We can stand it for a while, can't we?'

The heat, or the noise, or the sherry, or a combination of all three was making Alan's head spin. He was having difficulty in bringing objects into focus. Jane's white face and huge staring eyes were just a blur. Jimmy dumped two cups and two saucers full of coffee on the table and returned for his own. Alan unwrapped the sodden cube of sugar and let it slide slowly from the paper like thick granuled mud.

'That's seven pence you owe me,' Jimmy said.

'Scrooge!' Alan felt in his pocket. Someone opened the door and let in a draught of cold air to blow the fog from his eyes. Jane's lips were drawn tight. Bloodless. She looked sick. The dog whined. Alan leant across the table.

'Jane? Are you all right?'

The music was so loud he could hardly hear his own voice. Jane gripped the edge of the table with whitened knuckles and stared at the juke-box behind him.

'They don't need it,' Jane said.

Jimmy stirred his coffee and watched her, her long honey-brown hair. He was nearer to her. Caught the words over the wail of sound.

'They don't need it. They don't need that machine. Outside they used their voices to sing. They don't need machines to sing for them, talk for them. One day they'll have forgotten how. Their vocal cords will wither away. Don't they know what they're doing? They give machines the power to speak and one day they won't be able to speak, or sing. Machines will do it for them. Don't they know that? Don't they realise?'

'Jane?' Alan said again. She put her hands over her ears. Alan saw the red jagged scar where the rabbit had bitten her.

'I can't stand it,' Jane said. 'The noise. The awful noise. Machine noise. I can't bear it. Turn it off! Turn it off!'

Her eyes were fixed on the juke-box. People broke her line of vision but her eyes never moved. They grew hard. Hatred and fear poured from them. And power.

'Turn it off!' Jane shrieked.

Jimmy's chair crashed to the floor. The coffee cup tipped over spilling a stream of thick brown liquid across the red table top.

'Get her out of here,' Jimmy said wildly.

Alan jumped to his feet. Jane was going to be sick. There was a flash behind him, reflected in the mirror on the opposite wall. Someone screamed. The music stopped suddenly and a hot, strong smell filled the room, choking smoke, burning, pouring down his throat. People coughed and screamed and blundered into him. The door swung open. Hot smoke billowed out, cold rushed in. Jane and the pug forced a way through the crowd and out into the night.

'By heck,' Jimmy said. 'It blew up. The juke-box blew up.'

Alan found Jane leaning against the wall looking up at the sky.

'Feeling better?' Alan asked.

She nodded.

'Come on. I'll take you home.'

He took her arm and crossed the street to the place where he'd left his car. He could feel her shaking and hear the rattle of the pug's claws on the stone. The moon was riding bright and high. The air was bitter. Alan fitted the key in the lock and opened the door. Jimmy took the dog from Jane and bundled it behind the seat.

'Get in,' Jimmy told her. She was staring silently up at the sky, drained, exhausted. She felt empty. She needed to see the stars and gather strength. Replace the energy that was gone.

'Get in,' Jimmy said roughly and pushed her inside. He slammed the door loudly.

'What's biting you?' Alan asked.

'Her,' Jimmy said.

'What's she done?'

'It was her. She blew it up.'

'Don't be daft, man. She was nowhere near it.'

'She said turn it off.'

'So why didn't you?'

'Don't be daft, man,' Jimmy told himself. 'She was nowhere near it. It was her, though. She did it.'

7

Two strands of barb. Jimmy drove the staple in. Ought to keep the tats out.

There were pieces of wool caught on the thorns where they'd come through the gap in the hedge. Polished off Granny's cabbages, and all the brussels Jane had planted back in the summer. He tightened the wire round the end post. Nearly too dark to see. Sheep's wool hanging white, snow lying white, piled in drifts under the walls. No wind. A few melting drips off the roof. Silence everywhere. There was a break in the clouds overhead, with one star shining through. The sound of Jimmy's hammer rang hard on the metal, like a church bell, ding, ding, ding. Someone died. Morbid. That star was like an eye watching him.

Jimmy glanced behind him. Only the dark looming and the quiet snow, and the lights of the cottage behind closed curtains. Granny Bates watching the telly downstairs, Jane swotting upstairs. That girl was always swotting. Why couldn't she have asked someone else to mend the flipping fence? He remembered then she'd asked him months ago. Ding, ding, ding. The wire was strung taut. There was a flash when he hit it, a tiny spark. A spark of fire without any warmth. His fingers were so cold he could hardly feel them. Jimmy blew on his hands.

The door opened and a flood of light streamed out on to the path. Granny come to say she'd brewed up? Jimmy gave the post a final clout, sinking it deeper into the earth to hold the wire. A hot strong smell drifted round him.

'Jimmy!'

It was a cracked, pathetic call. Jimmy flung down the hammer and charged through the cabbage stumps and gooseberry bushes. Snow crept cold over the top of his boots and the smell of heat was stronger. Jane was standing in the doorway, leaning against it. Her face was white, drained, and her huge eyes were swimming with tears. The heat was intense.

'Jane! Jane, what is it girl?'

'Jimmy!' She leant her head against the door and started sobbing. Jimmy put his arm round her. He felt awkward. All those years he'd walked home with her and he'd never touched her. At least he couldn't remember touching her. Her hair felt just like fur; warm, soft and smooth.

'What is it then?' Just Jane's dry sobbing and the smell of heat.

'Jane?'

'I didn't mean to. I told her to turn it off. It was so loud. It was flickering and buzzing and it was so loud. She was just sitting there. That's all she ever does; sits there watching. I told her to turn it off. I didn't think she would. She never has before. I tried not to . . . but I couldn't help it. I didn't see her right by it, touching it. Jimmy I didn't want to. It just went.'

He pushed her aside. What had happened to upset Jane? Jane was crying. She'd never cried before. Not even when she slipped down the slope into a gorse bush and got prickles in her backside. She never cried about anything.

He went down the dingy passage to the living-room. The heat was overpowering. The smell of it suffocating. The smoke burning; not acrid, just hot. Jimmy choked and groped for the window. Flung it open and leaned out to breathe. Snow showered from the roof.

The curtains billowed inwards with the draught. Jimmy saw the smoke making blue spirals and curls around the light.

The sting in his eyes eased. Granny Bates was on the floor by the television. Her eyes were open. Her face was blue. Her hands clawed at her chest and her breathing came slow and noisy. Jimmy ran. Jane was still standing in the doorway.

'Out of the way,' Jimmy said. 'I'll fetch a doctor.'

The darkness blinded him. He slithered down the path to the gate. It was starting to snow again, huge silent white flakes drifting down. Doctor, had to get a doctor. He made for the telephone kiosk, then changed his mind. Nick was home. He'd noticed his car when he came by. Nick was a doctor. He'd know. The snow was deep, wet and slushy. His socks were soaked. He gave up trying to run. Dragged at his legs to make gigantic strides, deep black imprints on the smooth white surface. It was like running in a nightmare. There was glue on the road and his feet wouldn't go. But it wasn't a nightmare demon chasing him; it was the darkness and Granny Bates lying ill on the floor.

There was an old coaching lantern over the front door of Amberley House, camouflaging an electric light bulb. Jimmy's legs were aching as he hammered the knocker. The orange front-room curtain flickered with firelight. A wireless was going somewhere. Granny Bates was ill! Come on! Come on, will you! Jimmy used his fist as well and almost fell when the door opened suddenly.

'Well, come in,' Alan said.

'Nick!' Jimmy gasped. 'Get Nick quick!'

'What's the matter?'

'Get Nick. Granny Bates . . .'

'Nick!' Alan shouted. 'What's happened?'

'She's on the floor. I was mending the fence. Jane called

me. Granny's had some sort of attack.'

'Hello Jim,' Nick said from the living-room. 'Come on in.'

'Nick, can you come?' Alan asked. 'Jane's Gran . . . Jimmy thinks she's had a heart attack or something.' Nick murmured something over his shoulder, came into the hall and reached for his coat. Alan was half-way into his.

'When did this happen?' Nick asked Jimmy.

'Just now. I came straight here.'

'Have you rung her own doctor?'

'No. He'd have to come from Little Barton. That's five miles. Up Green Bottom in this weather could take him hours.'

'Fair enough. My bag's in the car. Fetch it would you, Alan. I'll just get my boots.'

'I'll get back,' Jimmy said.

'I'll be right behind,' Nick said.

'Where's Jane now?' Alan asked as he crossed to the car.

'She's there,' Jimmy told him. 'I'll get back.'

Jane was sitting on the settee, holding Winston. She was staring at the blank television screen. Jimmy watched her for a moment. The way she stared was uncanny. The fire had gone out and the room was cold. Jimmy shivered and closed the window.

'Jane?' If she heard him she gave no sign. No movement in her grey, staring eyes. Her white face was perfectly still, a statue carved from marble. Jimmy switched on the television. It was dead and the metal knob was hot. It burnt his fingers. The whole set was hot. Smelling hot. Jimmy went through to the kitchen for a knife.

Alan was making tea. Outside, the ambulance doors

57

slammed shut. The engine revved and there was a soft sound of wheels on the snow. The kitchen clock said five to eight. Two hours had seemed like eternity. Nick came in banging his hands together.

'Brr! Tea . . . just what I could do with. Where's Jane?'

'In the other room,' Jimmy said. 'Sitting.'

Alan poured out.

'Put two spoonsful of sugar in Jane's,' Nick said.

'She doesn't take sugar.'

'Sugar is good for shock.'

Alan spooned in two and stirred it. Jimmy needed something to undo the screws. He hunted through the table drawer.

'How old is she?' Nick asked.

''Bout sixty-five,' Jimmy said.

'No. Jane.'

'Fifteen,' Alan told him.

'She can't stay here on her own,' Nick said.

'She can have our spare room,' Alan offered.

'And afterwards? Next week? Next month? A stroke nearly always leaves its mark . . . blindness, degeneration, paralysis partial or total, and there's always a risk she'll have another. Granny Bates will be in hospital a long time, maybe for the rest of her life. That leaves Jane on her own. What about her mother?' The question was directed at Jimmy. He tested the blade of a vegetable knife. Ought to be strong enough.

'She hasn't got a Mam.'

'She has somewhere.'

'She went after Jane was born. Me Mam says she went to America. Or Australia. I'm not sure. I can ask me Mam. I don't think she even writes.'

'And her father?'

'I dunno.'

58

'Would your mother know?'

'Me Mam says it was a salesman. It weren't a salesman she went abroad with though. That my tea?'

'Yes,' Alan said. 'And that's Jane you're talking about, not someone from the *News of the World*.'

'It's not my fault her Mam walked out, nothing to do with me,' Jimmy said. 'I was still in nappies. Tough on her, though. And old man Bates popping off like that. Granny's got old since he went.'

'I'll contact the welfare people,' Nick said. 'They'll find a place for her in one of their homes or foster her out.'

'Why don't you just wrap her in newspaper and dump her outside the council offices?' Alan asked. 'After all, it's nothing to do with us, is it? Why don't we just buzz off home and leave her to sort things out for herself?'

He picked up Jane's tea and kicked open the door.

'Have you sugared mine?' Jimmy asked him.

'Sugar your own flaming tea. You and Dr Dolittle make me feel sick. That's Jane in there. Don't you feel anything, either of you—' A draught whistled through the kitchen. Cold and damp and smelling of drains.

'Hell,' Jimmy said. 'What a horrible thing to happen.'

'For Jane it's a tragedy,' Nick said quietly.

'What if Granny Bates dies?'

'I don't know. Maybe they'll be able to trace her parents. In any case she can stay with us until things get sorted out. Brr! Let's go into the other room. It's perishing in here.'

Nick glanced round the kitchen.

'It's a dump,' Jimmy said. 'I never realised before what a dump it was. That window's been broken for ages. I've been meaning to mend it. The gutter leaks down the wall. That's what makes all that damp. I said I'd mend that too. They didn't know how, Jane and Granny. But I never did it. It makes me feel like a rat.'

59

Nick rested a hand on his shoulder.

'If it's a dump, Jimmy, it's not your fault.'

Jimmy clutched his tea, dragging the warmth into his hands. It spilled hot on his fingers when he carried it in. Jane was still clutching the dog, still staring at nothing. Her tea stood untouched on the grimy arm of the sofa. Alan was looking worried.

'She doesn't seem to hear a word I say.'

Nick took Winston away from her and put him on the floor.

'Come on now, Jane. You can't sit here staring into space. Drink your tea.' He put the chipped cup in her hands. She sipped obediently.

'That's a good lass. Go on, now. Finish it. Then I think we'd better take you home and put you to bed. I've something that will make you sleep.'

Jimmy was working on the television. The screws turned easily. He knew what he'd find but he wanted to make sure. It was the same as the other times. In Alan's kitchen, in the café. The same smell of heat; heat powerful enough to melt solid metal in a single flash. Jane had told her to turn it off. Every time Jane said to turn it off. Then it blew up. Only this time Granny Bates had been touching it and she'd had a stroke. Poor old faggot. The whole idea was crazy. But it was right. He knew it was right. The last screw gave.

'All gone?' Nick said. 'Come on, then. You can stay with us for tonight.'

Jimmy pulled the back away. Heat drifted out in a wave, the smell of hot metal cooling, molten metal hardening. It was a twisted mass of metal parts fused together.

'Alan will fetch your coat,' Nick said to Jane. 'Where is it?'

Across the top of the television Jimmy stared at Jane.

Blue eyes and grey eyes holding a stare.

'You!' Jimmy said.

'No!'

'You!'

'No. It wasn't me.'

'You blew it up.'

'NO!'

'Yes you did. The washing machine. The juke-box. Now this. Your Gran was touching it and you blew it up. *Your Gran! You* did it.'

'No! I didn't! It wasn't me! It wasn't me! It wasn't!' She picked up the pug and ran from the room. They heard her running down the hallway sobbing. They heard the outside door open, felt the cold silence rush in. Nick looked at Jimmy.

'She couldn't take it, Jimmy. And right now nor can I.'

Alan followed Nick out. Jimmy stayed for a moment alone in the empty room. He shouldn't have said that. She couldn't take it. But it was her. She'd done it. She'd blown up the television. How? He put the knife on the sideboard and switched out the light.

The snow was deeper and still falling. It was very dark and very quiet. Even their own footsteps could hardly be heard. Just soft treads compressing the snow. Jane had gone somewhere, out in the night, swallowed up by the cold silent darkness.

'Hell!' Jimmy muttered. 'I'm sorry. Oh hell! Where's she gone?'

Alan started walking, head bent, straining to see the ground through the falling snow. He found where her footprints left the road and walked blindly down through the trees he only sensed were there, invisible pillars holding up the heavy sky. The silence closed round him and the clouds let down their feather flakes of snow. The loneliness was awful. How must Jane feel?

'Do you know where you're going?' Nick shouted. He found her footprints again and knew where she was going.

Alan stopped at the top of the quarry path where it dived steeply down to go round the bottom of Elgin. Below he saw a square of yellow light appear, a door being opened. He saw someone go in, a girl carrying a dog, just dark shapes through the pattern the snowflakes made. The door shut and everything was dark again.

'She's gone into the Battery House,' Alan said.

'Thank God for that,' Nick remarked.

'Shall we go down?'

'I will,' Nick said. 'I'd better tell the lady what's happened and make sure Jane is all right. You two go on home.' He went down the path.

'I'd like to punch you on the nose,' Alan said to Jimmy.

8 ·

I T gave Jimmy a sense of power carrying the gun. He
had cleaned the rust from the barrel and it gleamed like
new metal. The sun dragged the damp from the grass
and his feet made a squelching sound, disturbed the
trembling beads of dew that hung on every blade. The
larches were beginning to show green. There were catkins
on the birches that crowned the top of Winnard's Leap,
jackdaws building nests on the shallow ledges of the
quarry face. Jimmy stood on the edge of Elgin, looking
down over the hills bursting from winter into spring. His
eyes were keen, like a bird of prey searching for a movement below him, searching for a reason to use the rifle he
carried under his arm.

Alan, wearing his duffle coat, sweated in the damp
heat of the sun. Langdon Woods were grey-green on the
other side of the valley. He saw a flight of birds going
quick-winged across the sky.

'Pigeons,' Alan said. 'Go on, Jimmy. Pigeon pie.'

Jimmy moved the gun. It was poised ready. Aimed, not
at the sky, but at the quarry floor, the smooth amphi-
theatre of grass and small curls of springing bracken.
Nothing moved.

'I'm not after pigeons,' Jimmy said.

'I thought you were.'

'Changed me mind.'

'Not pigeons?'

'Rabbits.'

Alan laughed. 'Bet you fifty new pence you don't
catch one.'

'Make it two pence and you're on.'

'Done. Where did you unearth that relic?'

Jimmy ran his fingers in a caress over the carved butt.

'I was clearing out our Uncle Art's shed. Found it in the old copper. He said I could have it. Cleaned up well it did.'

'It might fetch a good price in a junk shop,' Alan remarked. 'Some people pay a lot for antique firearms. They collect them.'

'It's not that old.'

'With a carved butt? Must be. Dropped in the Wars of the Roses, probably.'

Jimmy didn't mind if it was old. It was a gun. *His* gun. For once he had something Alan didn't have. He went on down the quarry path. What he wanted now was a rabbit. There used to be rabbits down Langdon Point. He remembered seeing their droppings when he and Stan Potter had gone that way a couple of summers back. Langdon Point was a long way into the hazy distance but it would be worth going there to shoot a rabbit, and have Alan watch him. The hills closed round them and took away the view. Small streams of water ran chuckling between the stones of the path heading for Green Bottom. The black clouds of the morning had turned to a hot blue sky, but rain still showered from the oak tree overhanging the fork.

'Wow!' Jimmy said. 'Look at that.' On the grass opposite the Battery House a girl in a scarlet dress was kneeling. Her hair was long and brown; honey lights glinting in the sun. Jimmy stood still on the path under the dripping oak tree and gave a piercing whistle. She was watching the ground and did not look round.

'Try calling her,' Alan said. 'Jane! Hey, Jane! Where have you been all this time?' Jimmy stared. That wasn't Jane. It couldn't be. Jane didn't look like that. Jane

64

wasn't pretty and that girl was. Even without seeing her face Jimmy knew she was pretty. Alan went down.

'Jane!'

The earth was running through her fingers: warm, soft, high smelling, rich dark-brown. The earth smelled of spring and things beginning to grow. The small stones as she moved them shone, tiny crystals catching the sun, changing them from grey rock to topaz and amethyst. Rain hung like liquid emeralds on the grass, or like diamonds on the withered leaves. She was part of the spring, in it, above it, under it, over it. It was all round her. She could smell it, see it, hear it, and touch it, rich spring earth crumbling through her fingers.

'Jane!' Alan said.

She turned and smiled.

'Hello, Alan.'

Jimmy stood over her, looking down. Blue shadow and black mascara accentuated her huge grey eyes. There was a smudge of soil on her cheek.

'Bates! What have you done to yourself?'

'Hi, Keir. I haven't done anything.'

'Yes you have. Your hair. Make-up. That dress!'

Jane glanced down at her scarlet dress.

'It's a new one. I got it in Paris.'

'You what?' Jimmy said.

'Paris. You know. Paris, France. We spent two days there. Then we went to a fishing village called Saint Marie de la Mare. It was super. And there was an island where we went for the day. It was like a desert island. Sand dunes and rough grass. We visited some chateaux too . . .'

'Hang on,' Jimmy said. 'Are you saying you've just been to France?'

'Of course I have.'

'*She* took you?'

65

'Yes.'

'Our Mam never told me.'

'Marcia's been before. She can speak French fluently. She bought herself one of those ghastly berets. It makes her look a frump. I wanted her to have a straw hat. She looked much nicer in a straw hat.'

'Marcia? Is that her name? The bat-woman?'

'She's not a bat,' Jane said. 'She's good and kind. She took me on holiday. She's bought me everything I ever wanted. She's not a bat.'

'No,' Alan said. 'No. She's not a bat. When did you go?'

'The day before Good Friday.'

'Two weeks in France,' Jimmy muttered. 'By heck! If some people fell off a cliff they'd land on a feather bed. Struck oil, haven't you?'

'What's that supposed to mean?'

'It means you could have landed in a welfare home. Play your cards right and she'll leave you all her money when she pops off.'

Jane's eyes clouded.

'Oh shut up!' Alan said. 'I'm sorry about your Gran, Jane.' She had died a week before Easter. Marcia had taken her on holiday but she couldn't forget. Jimmy had forgotten but Jane couldn't. 'Your Gran was touching it and you blew it up. You did it. Your Gran. You did it.' Why had Jimmy said that? She'd heard him saying it a thousand times whilst Gran was ill. Those words over and over again and she didn't know why. She trickled the soil through her fingers, but all the magic was gone. The spring had lost its intensity.

'We had the welfare people round the day after Gran died,' Jane said. 'Marcia had to sign some forms. I'm to stay with her.'

'She'll look after you,' Alan said.

'Yes,' Jane said bleakly. 'She'll look after me.'

A white pug came from behind the wall, yapped at Jimmy and Alan and started digging in Jane's hole.

'Which one's that?' Jimmy asked.

'Mine.'

'Where's t'other?'

'With Marcia. Randolph's hers. Winston's mine.' Soil flew between Winston's hind legs.

'What were you grubbing for, anyway?' Jimmy asked.

A blackbird flew through the trees with a cry of alarm. Sun came through the branches of the tree, shone on the stones and on Jane's honey-brown hair.

'Marcia found the rabbit,' Jane said. 'She went back the next day and found it in the bracken where you threw it. She cut it up. She found them in there. That's how she knows. Then she buried it. Somewhere under a stone but she can't remember where.'

'Found what in the rabbit?' Alan asked. Jane frowned. Trying to remember.

'I don't know. It bit me. It bit Winston too.'

'And you're trying to dig up a rabbit's corpse?' Jimmy's voice was scornful.

'It'll be bones by now,' Alan said.

'Marcia said she was sorry. She didn't know they were still inside. She thought she'd found them all. But there are still some buried somewhere. Trapped under the earth. I can't just leave them there.'

'What?' Alan asked.

Again Jane frowned.

'I don't know,' she said slowly.

'You're both bats,' Jimmy said. 'You and Fatty Cotterel. A right flipping pair. Mad as coots. Digging up dead rabbits. Now I've heard it all.'

Jane stared at him, huge grey eyes hurt and puzzled. Then her eyes moved to the rifle, the long shining barrel.

Machines which could kill were the worst of all. But then every machine could kill. Quickly, with force and fire. Slowly with fumes, gases, noise, strangulation of the mind. That silent rifle was hardly a machine but it could still kill. Jimmy could kill, a small brown rabbit with a hurt leg. Jimmy shifted uneasily. He wished he hadn't said that.

'Come for a walk,' Jimmy said.

'I can't. We're going out soon.'

'Tomorrow then.'

'I think we're going out tomorrow too.'

'Oh, get lost,' Jimmy said. 'Come on,' he said to Alan. Then he hesitated. Jane was pretty. She was suddenly pretty. 'There's a dance on next Saturday,' Jimmy said to Jane. 'Come with me.'

'I can't,' Jane said again.

'Why not? Not going with Fanny every day are you?'

'Marcia goes to Bristol on Saturday evenings. To a scientists' meeting. She's never home before one.'

'Then you can come with me.'

'No. I can't.'

'Why?'

'Because I can't.'

'Why? Go on, tell me why. Isn't Hasley town hall good enough for you after the Eiffel Tower?'

'It's not that.'

'Aren't I good enough? I suppose you'd rather have a Frenchman with a yacht?'

'No ... Jimmy ...'

'If *he*'d asked you it would have been different, wouldn't it? You'd have gone like a shot if Alan had asked you. He's got a white car.'

'Belt up!' Alan said. 'If she doesn't want to go that's reason enough.'

'I want to know why,' Jimmy demanded. Jane backed

towards the gate.

'Why won't you go with me? Come on, Bates. Answer!'

'Because I'm not allowed out in the dark,' Jane choked and ran up the path.

Jimmy clutched the rifle, staring after her, at the bungalow, El Garda hanging over the door in wrought-iron letters.

'What's she mean . . . she's not allowed out after dark?'

'Perhaps she means what she says,' Alan said crossly. 'Why don't you keep your mouth shut. She was crying.'

The pug was sitting on the path, fixing them with a basilisk stare.

'And all that dribble about rabbits.'

'For Pete's sake come on.'

There were new shutters fixed outside the laboratory windows, bolts gleaming on the door.

'What is that place?' Jimmy demanded. 'A concentration camp?'

The April day was going to dark. The cluster of cottages in Green Bottom showed their lights and the lights from the Battery House fell across the front lawn. It was a damp, hot twilight and the rumbles of hunger in Alan's stomach sounded like thunder. He ducked wearily under the wire fence that bordered the railway line and took the tiny steep path down the side of the quarry. He reached the road with dragging feet. Up over Elgin and home.

'Our Mam will be right chuffed,' Jimmy said for the twentieth time. 'Pity I didn't stick at fifty.' He was carrying the gun in one hand and a pair of rabbits in the other. He carried them with pride. Something Alan couldn't have done, shot two rabbits.

'The next time you might tell me,' Alan muttered.

'And I'll bring my flipping tea.'

'You hungry, boyo?'

'Yes. As it happens I am.'

'Worth it, though. Two rabbits. Worth missing tea.'

'For you maybe.'

Off in the brown decaying tangle of last year's bracken a night-jar gave its eerie rattle. A sheep with two lambs scuttered across the road, stared at them both with offended eyes and proceeded to feed her young. Two black tails waggled furiously. The side door of the Battery House opened suddenly and a bar of yellow light flooded the path. Alan stumbled over a stone under the oak tree.

'Shut up!' Jimmy said viciously.

'You . . .'

'Shut up! Look! There's Brainy Bates.'

In the still evening her voice came clearly.

'Can't I stay up? Just this once?'

'No, you can't. I'm sorry, but you can't.'

'Please, Marcia. Just once. Just this one time.'

'Now come along, Jane. It's for your own good.'

Jane and Miss Cotterel were in the kitchen.

'But why?' Jane wailed. 'Why can't I stay up? I could stay with you. Watch the telly. Why can't I?'

'You know why, dear. I told you why. We agreed, didn't we? We agreed this was the best way.'

She was gripping Jane's arm. Leading her along the path between the lawns, along to the laboratory at the bottom of the garden with its bolts and shutters. Jane began to struggle.

'Don't lock me in! I don't want to be locked in! Let me go! Please let me go!' Alan and Jimmy were watching.

'I'll knock her block off,' Jimmy said angrily.

Inside the lights came on. They could see Jane through the window, sitting on the bed, her face covered with her hands. They saw Miss Cotterel bending over her, patting her shoulder, talking to her; then she drew the curtains, came out and shut the door. They heard the bolts being drawn. They watched her fastening the white-wood shutters until the last glow of light behind the curtained windows was gone.

'Are we just going to stand here and watch?' Jimmy asked. 'That's Jane in there. That old cow's locked her in.'

Miss Cotterel and one white pug walked back up the path.

'Locked her in with them bats,' Jimmy said furiously.

'I didn't see any bats,' Alan said slowly. 'It looked to me as if it's been converted to a bedroom.'

'But Jane didn't want to go. You heard her. She didn't want to go and that old faggot made her.'

Alan turned to go.

'What's the matter, boy? That night Granny Bates was took bad you were charging round on your white horse. Now Jane's locked in there you don't want to know. All talk and no do, that's your trouble, mate.'

'She's given her a good home,' Alan said. 'She's looked after her. Jane herself said that. You can't go tearing in there and tell her to let Jane out.'

'Good home? Locking Jane in the potting shed? That's giving her a good home? More like Holloway.'

'Well, go on then. Go and knock at the door. Tell Miss Cotterel you don't think Jane's being treated properly. Go on. What are you waiting for?'

There was a glimmer of starlight, a faint breath of wind through the branches of the oak tree, a faint touch of coldness to remind Jimmy it was not yet summer. He was hungry and he had two rabbits to take home.

'Skip it,' Jimmy muttered.

'You're not leaving her in there?'

'It's late.'

'You're leaving her? After all you said?'

'Oh, come on. I'm hungry.'

'All talk was it, Jimmy?'

'You'll say one word too much one day. Put a sock in it.'

'I thought it was only talk.'

Jimmy gritted his teeth.

'For your information, boyo, Jane's coming to that dance next week. The old bag goes out on Saturdays, so I'll let her out. And you can come and watch me do it.'

'If you do,' Alan said amiably, 'I'll take you to Hasley in my car.'

Jane pulled back the curtains and saw the shutters outside the glass. Soon the sky would be heavy with stars revolving in the silent depth of space. She had been glad to leave them, but she still needed them. She needed their power. Marcia understood so much, why could she not understand that? Why did she shut her away from the stars? Without them she could only half exist, like sleeping, existing without being aware.

Winston whined at the door and scratched to go out. Jane picked him up, sinking her face against his fur, knowing he felt as she did the terrible longing to see the stars.

9

'WHERE'VE you left the car?' Jimmy asked. 'I hope you had the gump to put it somewhere she won't see it.'

'It's on one of those tracks going into Langdon Woods, the other side of the bridge.'

'Good boy. She shouldn't go that way anyway if she's going to Bristol.'

'It's eight o'clock,' Alan said. 'How long are we waiting here?'

They were in a hollow in the hills, a little enclave which hid them from the world. There was only the pale April sky above, growing a little dreary, and the tops of the birch trees above Winnard's Leap. Jimmy brushed a few pieces of bracken from his maroon trousers, and straightened his pink floral tie.

'We'll go on down,' Jimmy said. 'We can keep an eye on the Battery House from that path going into Elgin. We'll be able to see when she goes.'

'And if she decides to take the dogs for a walk before she goes, and sees us?'

'Well, we're not committing a crime, are we? We can go for a walk too, can't we? It's National Trust property. Not private or anything.'

'In these clothes?' Alan asked, looking down at his own dark suit, white shirt and black tie.

'I should have told you it wasn't a hunt ball we were going to,' Jimmy remarked. 'Never mind. If she asks, you've just come from a funeral.' He wound his way between the hills, taking the narrow sheep paths, crossing the main path, up over the steep slope which bounded Elgin and reached the top. There was the land below all the way to Hasley. The Battery House was in darkness.

'She's gone,' Jimmy said. 'The laboratory's shuttered. She must have put Jane to bed early.'

'Maybe Jane doesn't want to come,' Alan said doubtfully.

'She does,' Jimmy said. 'I asked her again. She wanted to come. She said she'd be ready if we let her out.'

'I don't like it. Miss Cotterel's looking after Jane as she thinks right.'

'Right? You call that sort of looking after her right? Jane's nearly sixteen. She's put to bed at eight o'clock and locked in. She ought to have some freedom. She says she wants to come to the dance. OK. She's coming. If you don't like it you can go. I'll bring Jane on the bus. There's one in twenty minutes.'

Alan slithered down the slope.

'You're coming then?'

'Yes.'

The gate creaked as he opened it. The garage was shut.

'Fanny Cotterel could be having a bath,' Alan said.

'Try ringing the doorbell,' Jimmy suggested.

'What for?'

'To see if she answers it.'

'And if she does?'

'We'll know she's still here. Tell her we're collecting for the R.S.P.C.A. She might cough up ten pence.'

Alan pressed the orange glowing electric bell. There was a shrill ringing from inside. One of the dogs started barking. Alan rang again.

'She's out,' Jimmy said. 'Come on.' They went down the garden to the laboratory. Jimmy drew back the bolts and opened the door. Jane was wearing her jade-green

74

coat. She had pinned up her hair and made up her face. Jimmy was glad he'd asked her.

'Ready?'

Alan was waiting on the lawn. Daffodils sported heavy golden heads in flower borders. Dew was falling fast; so was the dark. Jane didn't notice him. She was clutching Jimmy's hand, her grey eyes glowing with excitement.

'I thought you were never coming. Marcia went ages ago.'

'We shan't have missed much,' Jimmy said. 'It won't liven up till later. Come on then, girl. Put that flipping dog inside and let's go.'

'I'm bringing him,' Jane said.

'You what?'

'I'm bringing him. He wants to come.'

'Swipe me! You can't take a dog dancing.'

'I can't leave Winston behind. He wants to come.'

'You can leave him in the car,' Alan offered. 'He'll be OK. We can shut the windows.'

Jimmy stalked off down the path muttering. Alan closed the door and bolted it. 'Just in case she comes back before we do.'

Jane smiled. 'Thank you for letting me bring Winston.'

'All part of the service, lady.'

She laughed, and saw the first pale gleam of stars.

Jane was in among the music, in among the people, a swaying, seething mass of bodies moving to the rhythm. Jimmy was in front of her, shaking his hips, his legs, his hands. Turning, backing, coming again. Tight maroon trousers, flowered tie. A blurred face with falling hair. If she stood still she could see he was Jimmy, smiling in approval at her short turquoise dress, black patent shoes and gold gypsy earrings. But when she moved the room was just a blur, everyone in it was a blur, there was only

75

the music and the dancing.

'I didn't know you liked dancing,' Jimmy said. Jane's skirt swirled round. Her black shoes sparkled. Her earrings made a jangling noise.

'You're great. I didn't know you could dance.'

Turn and come again.

'Why didn't you say? I'd have brought you before.'

It was like dancing on a cloud. She couldn't feel the floor.

'We could come again next week.'

The music stopped, then started again. It was strange. Jane had never liked dancing before. She'd never been able to move in time with the music. But now it caught her, the beat pulsated through her like blood through her veins: smooth, rhythmical, powerful. She could hear it in her head, hear it in the stamping of her feet. She gave herself to it completely: music, rhythm, dancing feet.

She danced because she *had* to dance, because *they* wanted her to dance. They were enclosed in her mind, co-ordinating her steps, controlling the movements of her muscles with perfect timing, making her give herself to the rhythm. They shared her enjoyment, her wildness, her abandonment. Jane danced for them. She was not aware of the circle of people who watched her and Jimmy dance.

She danced for nearly an hour. She danced non-stop, hands meeting Jimmy's hands, backing away, hands meeting again. She breathed to the music, lived with the music, moved to the music. Then it stopped. People clapped all around her. Jane felt bewildered, as if she had just been woken from sleep.

Jimmy put his arm round her waist.

'Girl, you were absolutely great. I didn't know you could dance like that. We showed them how, Jane. You and me. We showed them how to dance.' The music came again, slower, couples dancing closely together under dimmed lights.

'Again?' Jimmy asked.

Jane was trying to regain her breath.

'Let's sit this one out. I'll get you a Coke. You've earned it.' Jane nodded and went to a table. She was restless now. The music meant nothing, just a clatter of sound without any rhythm, without the swaying compulsion which made her want to dance. She sipped the luke-warm drink Jimmy brought her.

'Well, say something,' Jimmy said. 'Say you're enjoying it.'

'I am.'

'You're glad you came?'

'Yes.'

'Glad we let you out, even if she does find out?'

'It doesn't matter if she does.'

'No,' Jimmy agreed. 'It doesn't matter if she does because if she gets nasty I'll belt her one.'

'It doesn't matter because it's too late,' Jane said. 'It's dark. Marcia can't stop me now.'

'Stop you?'

Jane looked startled. 'It's hot in here.'

'Uh huh. There's Alan with Caroline Hunt.'

Jane stared at the brown liquid in the glass. It was hot. She wanted to go out. She wanted to go out into the dark.

'Drink up,' Jimmy said. 'We'll show them how again.'

The music still meant nothing. Nothing to dance to. It was only noise going on and on. Her limbs were stiff and awkward. There was no flow, no giving way, only a longing to go outside.

'Put some life into it,' Jimmy said.

'I'm trying.'

'What's the matter with you? You were great just now.'

'I'm tired.'

'Not already? You can't be. We've only been here an hour.'

Jane forced herself to move, to twist and turn, to shake. She was glad when the end came. Jimmy started talking football with Stan Potter. Jane was going to slip away, out into the quiet cool darkness. Jimmy caught her as she reached the door.

'Hey, come on. This is a twist.' She came reluctantly back to the noise. Jimmy waved his hands above his head and moved his hips.

'Twist!' Jimmy said.

Jane twisted. Knocked against a girl in a black skirt. Back and come again.

'Twist!' She was too slow. He lost the rhythm waiting for her to turn.

'Twist!' Jane whirled and swung inwards, collided with Jimmy as she turned.

'Wait for the music, you nit. Right. Now twist!' She went back, twisted, stepped towards him, clutched his hot sticky hand.

'Ow! My flipping foot.'

'Sorry Jimmy.'

The music went on, loud cymbals, loud drums. Jane's only thought was to reach the end and escape.

'You're dragging. You're not listening to the music. This is a twist, not a blooming military two-step.'

'I'm sorry.'

'Can't you say anything else besides sorry? You're waddling round like a stuffed duck. Pick your flipping feet up.'

Jane stood still.

'Don't just stand there. Dance!'

78

The dancers moved round them.

'You twerp!'

Jimmy scowled at her.

'Oh, let's give it a rest. I'm fed up. And don't start snivelling. If you want to dance again I'll be around somewhere.'

Jane crept from the hall. Jimmy always said something that hurt. Usually the truth. The coolness and darkness was relief. Jane looked up and forgot Jimmy. The stars were shining, hundreds and thousands of them, shining bright against the black sky. She ran to the car. It was locked, but that didn't matter. Winston would be able to see them through the window. Far, far away the music was playing. Far, far away the stars shone, the perfect shining beautiful stars. Jane leaned against the car door and watched them.

The church clock struck eleven-thirty.

'Why aren't you dancing?' Alan asked.

'Jimmy didn't like my dancing.'

'But you were good. I was watching you. Everyone was watching you.'

'That was at first. After that I wasn't good.'

'Have you been out here long?'

The frost had covered the car with white. It gleamed on the streets and on the pavements, on the roofs of the houses and in her hair. It reflected the street lights and in the dark places it reflected the stars. It was white on her sleeves, too. Jane brushed it away.

'Not long,' she said.

'You're shivering. I'll unlock the car and you can sit inside. I'll fetch your coat if you give me the ticket. Do you want to stay or go home?'

'Go,' Jane said.

'Fair enough. Where's Jimmy now?'

'Still dancing, I expect.'

'I'll find him and ask him if he wants to come. Shan't be long.'

Jane was shut in the car with Winston: a girl and a dog drunk with starlight. Winston licked her face. She knew he was happy. She was happy, too. In a minute Jimmy would come and say something nasty and make some of the happiness go. Alan brought her coat.

'Jimmy's not coming.' She was glad. Alan was glad, too.

'How will he get back?' Jane asked. 'The last bus has gone.'

'Stan Potter,' Alan said.

Jane struggled to find the sleeve of her coat. Alan held it for her. Frosted hair and fur collar on either side of his hand.

'Right,' Alan said. 'Off we go.'

'When we were in France,' Jane began, 'we went . . .'

She stiffened and fell silent. Alan had turned on the ignition, red ignition light, green oil light, soft purring engine. Winston whined miserably. Jane clutched him. Alan slid the car into gear.

'What were you saying?'

'Nothing,' Jane whispered.

The smell of petrol made her feel sick. The noise of the engine roared in her head, loud revs as they started off, a high-pitched whine as they went along the High Street. Lorries went past them buffeting the car with rushes of speed. They turned away from the South Wales road and headed for Langdon Forest. Trees made cathedral arches over the road and their trunks became white pillars in the stabbing headlamps. The road was empty and the car gathered speed.

Jane gritted her teeth. She could feel the vibrations and hear the air rushing by. She was engulfed and part of the machine. She couldn't do anything without it. Not move. Her legs were the wheels of the car. Not speak. Her voice was its whining engine. It was all around her encasing her mind in metal. She wanted to retaliate, blast it to pieces, escape from it. She wanted to pour out all the starlight her eyes had taken in and explode it. If she concentrated all her power on it . . . Jane clutched the side of the seat. Her own common sense took over. She couldn't do that. It was Alan's car.

The car rushed down the hill, through the sleeping village of Little Barton. Farm fields replaced the trees, then trees replaced the farm fields. Jane saw the green and yellow sign: Langdon Forest Park. The hills were steeper, more rugged, pitted with quarries. The road was never ending. At last there was the sharp bend where the railway embankment was shored up with a dry stone wall. The hills reared up on either side, utterly black. The beginning of Green Bottom. Not much farther. It would stop soon and let her out. She was still herself. She could move without the machine. She could talk and see and walk. It would let her out. Alan changed gear to take the hill. Marble cherubs with folded wings stood white among the gravestones in the stone works beside the road.

Alan slowed down by the post box, and the noise of the engine was gone. Jane breathed quietly and let her taut muscles relax. The strain of riding inside a machine was over. The strain of resisting it, controlling the power within her mind, was over. All the time she'd wanted to let go, a blast of heat, heat, force and power to melt the metal and free herself. She was cold with sweat.

'I'll walk you home,' Alan said.

'It's only just up the path.'

'I'll take you there. I ought to lock you in.'

'No,' Jane said.

He opened the door. Winston jumped out, and scampered like a white wraith up the path.

'You needn't bother to lock me in,' Jane said. 'Marcia probably won't notice. And if she does she'll think she forgot.'

'I'll come with you, anyway. You don't know who you might meet between here and there.'

The air was tangy with frost. It gleamed on the stones and the stars hung sharp over them. Jane stared up at them.

'She's not back yet,' Alan said. 'Or if she is she's in bed.'

The Battery House was in darkness.

'I don't want to go in yet,' Jane said.

'It's late. Almost midnight.' The green luminous hands of his watch said seven minutes to.

'She doesn't usually come in till about one. I want to go for a walk.'

'Now?'

'Yes.'

'Well, all right. Looks like that dog of yours is going anyway.'

Winston was a splash of white some way ahead snuffling among the bracken for smells to excite his nose: a woodmouse or a shrew or the earthy upheavals of a mole. All new and delicious. Too delicious to be left. Winston dug busily.

The moon was rising over the bank of clouds and hills, shining gold over Langdon Point, making the landscape weird with pools of light and shadow, silver with moonlight and frost. Gorse became spiky turreted castles with moats of darkness. Rocks gleamed like diamonds and took on a brief valueless beauty which would be gone by morning, washed away by the rain. Over the edge of Elgin the lights of Hasley gleamed like stars beside the silver river, snaking between silver hills.

'Magic,' Jane said. 'It's magic. If we jumped we'd fly.'

'You go first,' Alan said. 'I'll follow.'

She took a step nearer the edge. She was poised on the brink of a precipice with just blackness below. Alan caught her wrist.

'I didn't mean that.'

'I wasn't going to jump. I'm not daft. It's just that everything seems like a dream. You don't fall in dreams, do you? You just float on and on, dropping down and down and never reach the bottom.'

Alan squeezed her hand.

'It's not a dream, girl.'

'No. It's real. The dark's real. The stars are real.'

Alan looked up.

'Why does she lock you in?'

'Marcia you mean?'

'Yes. Why?'

'You wouldn't understand.'

'Try me.'

They were both looking up.

'It's the stars. Marcia says I mustn't see them.'

'Why not?'

'I don't know.'

'You must do. She must have a reason. She must have told you.'

'They're powerful,' Jane said. 'They're beautiful, and lonely, and powerful.'

Alan stared at her. 'They're millions of light years away.'

'But I can see them,' Jane said. 'I can see them. They're powerful.'

Alan shook his head. 'And she locks you in because she doesn't want you to look at the stars? She must be stupid.'

'Marcia's not stupid,' Jane denied. 'She's clever. She's much cleverer than me. She understands and she tries

83

to explain. She's so kind she nearly suffocates me. When she locks me in at night she's being kind, but sometimes I forget that. I scream at her to let me go. I hate her because she won't let me see the stars and I want to see them. After she's gone I'm always sorry I hated her.'

'OK,' Alan said. 'So she's kind. I'm not saying she's not. She's good to you. But I don't get it. What harm can stars do you?'

'Like moonlight,' Jane said.

'Moonlight?'

'The moon can make people go mad,' Jane said. 'They stare and stare at it until they go mad. It's a dead world of dust and rocks, utterly silent, but it drives people mad.'

Alan gripped her shoulders. Her eyes were luminous. Pools of moonlight. Moonlight could drive people mad. Moon crazy. That's where the word lunatic came from.

'You're not going mad,' Alan said. 'Is that what she thinks? That you're going mad?'

Jane laughed. Her laughter echoed round the cold hills. Then the silence came back and everything was still. Jane and Alan stood on top of Elgin for a magic unmoving moment of time. A car came up Green Bottom. The sound never reached them but Jane turned her head and broke the spell.

'Did you know that only human beings can make music?' Jane asked. 'Birds sing but we can make music. Strings or keys or breathing through a reed. Music is an expression of hearing, like painting is an expression of seeing. We're the only creatures who don't depend on our senses for survival, we use them only for pleasure.'

'What brought that on?' Alan inquired. 'I thought you didn't understand music? Have you undergone a sudden metamorphosis?'

'It's the stars,' Jane said. 'And the magic. I'll remember tonight for a long time because of the magic and the stars.'

'Not because of me?'

'Oh, and you too,' Jane said. She whistled softly. The white pug came running, and she scooped him up.

'I suppose the magic is over now?' Alan remarked.

'It's late,' Jane said. 'I'm going to bed.'

They went down the path together. Down and down. A motor bike on the road below roared by, a rip of sound through the night.

Jane stood still.

'Some people don't hear music,' she said. 'They only hear noise. And they never see anything, they only watch the telly. They never feel anything deep. They never use their senses at all. They never even think.'

'Sounds like Jimmy,' Alan said. 'He doesn't bother to think.'

Jane was gripping the gate.

'Jimmy knows,' Jane said.

'Yes,' Alan agreed. 'All about the innards of ten-ton lorries.'

'About me.'

'I'd noticed that. He knows a lot about you. How to make you miserable. What was it he called you? A stuffed duck?'

'He didn't mean it.'

'But he said it.'

'I'm going in now.'

'Don't go yet. Stay a bit longer.'

'Jimmy will be coming by in a minute.'

'Oh damn Jimmy!' Alan said.

Jane opened the gate.

'I'm going in.'

'I'm sorry,' Alan said. 'I shouldn't have said that.'

85

'I'm going.'

'I'll come and bolt the door.'

'No. Don't bother. She won't notice. She'll put the car away and go to bed.'

'Jane . . . wait!'

'Goodbye.'

'I didn't mean it. Jimmy's OK.'

'I'm not a stuffed duck,' Jane said. 'Jimmy didn't mean it, either.'

'Oh hell!' Alan muttered.

Jane went into the laboratory and closed the door.

IO

THE girl disintegrated, melted, became just a cloud of tiny cells, colourless as plasma, floating in the air and yet still in human shape. She was no longer tangible flesh and bone. She was merely a substance with no solid form. A clock started striking; loud solemn notes, one following the other. Six, seven, eight, nine, ten, eleven, twelve. Was it noon or midnight? Midnight, because the girl had gone. There were only stars whirling against black space. They kept no orbits. They moved and came together, taking shape. Becoming definite. A girl made out of stars. The echoes of the clock faded away. A door banged and a sudden light hurt Alan's eyes. He groaned.

'Are you staying in bed all day?' Nick asked as he drew back the curtains.

Alan rolled over, buried his face in the pillow to shut out the light. Being woken in the middle of a dream always made him bad-tempered.

'Go away!'

'Get up!'

'Go away and leave me alone. It's cruelty.'

'It's mid-day. Lunch will be ready in an hour.'

'Don't want any.'

It ought to mean something. A girl made out of stars. Against the blackness of his closed eyelids he could see her floating. If he got up now he would forget. He wanted to remember, cling to the drifting illusion and find a meaning.

'Let me go to sleep.'

'Get up,' Nick said harshly.

Alan tried to ignore him. To sink back into sleep. Turn

87

the daylight back into darkness again. Recapture the drifting floating drowsiness before it was gone.

'Get up!' Nick said quietly. 'Get up now!'

Alan opened his eyes. The grey daylight was dazzling. He could hear rain and see Nick standing over him, looking down. Nick's dark hair was beginning to go grey. There were wrinkles across his forehead and his eyes were hard, humourless, flinty blue. Nick was in one of his nasty moods.

'Get up!'

'I'm getting. I'm getting. What's the rush?'

'And dress yourself. You're not loafing round for hours in your dressing-gown.'

'But my dressing-gown is part of a Sunday morning tradition.'

'I said get dressed. It's Sunday afternoon, not Sunday morning. I make the traditions in this house.'

Alan sat up.

'Have I done something?'

'You're darned right you've done something.'

'Like what?'

'Like you disgust me. When you're ready come downstairs. I'm going before I leather you.'

Alan slid out of bed.

'What have I done?'

'I'll tell you downstairs when my temper's had ten minutes to cool off.'

Alan shrugged and fumbled with his shirt buttons. A wet sun came through the clouds. The wind was blowing drops off the roof. A few hours ago the world had been silver with frost, bright with moonlight and silent with magic. All the magic had gone. Nick was in an evil mood. What had he done?

The brown and gold carpet in the front room felt warm

88

under Alan's bare feet. A familiar sinking feeling. His mother had just lit the fire. Small sticks crackled with cold orange flames and blue smoke curled thickly up the chimney. The rain blew against the window, trickled down and caught the watery gleam of sun. The clock ticked monotonously. Alan took a cigarette from the packet on the piano and went to stand beside Nick and stare from the window.

'There's a rainbow.'

Nick looked grim.

'A rainbow and a cuckoo's song . . .'

'Never mind the cuckoo.'

Alan grinned.

'Take that smug smile off your face.'

'Suppose you tell me what I'm supposed to have done?'

'You really don't know?'

'No I don't,' Alan said hotly. 'I'm not a blasted mind-reader. How the hell am I supposed to know if you don't tell me?'

'Your language is deplorable.'

'Some people are annoying enough to make a parson swear.'

'I thought your mother had brought you up well.'

'Your high opinion of me is very flattering, Dr Spock.'

'Flattering! That's the last thing it was meant to be. I don't intend to flatter you. You have completely disgusted your mother and me. Your morals, my boy, leave much to be desired.'

'Can't you omit your sociological opinions, Grandad, and get to the point?'

'One more remark like that and you'll feel my hand. What time did you get in last night?'

'What is this? The Spanish Inquisition?'

'What time did you get in?'

'What's it to do with you? There's not a curfew on.'

89

'What time did you get in?'

'All right. Don't shout. Twelve-thirty. So what? Twenty to one. I don't know. I never looked.'

'You're lying.'

Alan clenched his fist.

'Give!'

'I'll give,' Nick said. 'You're lying, Alan.'

'Say that once more and I'm leaving home and getting a job. I got in around half past twelve.'

'So you intend to stick to your story?'

'It's not a story. I got in at half past twelve. Half past twelve. Just after. Fact.'

'Not half past four?'

'Come off it. You heard me. I put the car away.'

'Your mother and I went to bed early. I didn't hear you.'

'Then you'll just have to accept what I say, won't you? I was in bed before one.'

'And Jane?'

'What about Jane?'

'Did you bring her in with you?'

'What a vile insinuation.'

'Did you?'

'No I didn't.'

Nick lit a cigarette. The room was dark with shadow, loud with rain, quiet with tension.

'We had Miss Cotterel here about an hour ago,' Nick said.

'Oh yes?'

'She was threatening to fetch the police.'

'Oh yes?'

'She was hopping mad. Anna made her a cup of coffee and she was so furious she couldn't drink it. You know she's Jane's legal guardian now? That she's adopting

90

her? That the adoption papers are in the process of going through?'

'I didn't know she was adopting her. I do now. So what did she want?'

Nick ground out his cigarette and flung the butt in the grate. He swung round to face Alan with angry eyes.

'Jane got in at ten past four last night,' Nick said. 'Miss Cotterel waited up for her. Ten past four, Alan, and she said she was with you.'

Alan stared at Nick.

'She said what?'

'Jane said she was with you until ten past four.'

'And you believed her?'

'I didn't see Jane. Only Miss Cotterel. The woman is not a liar.'

'But I am?'

'I take it you're denying it?'

'You're darned right I am.'

'Then where was she?'

'I don't know but she wasn't with me. It was half past twelve when I left her. I watched her go in. You thought I brought Jane home with me? To spend the night? With you and Mum in the next room? You thought that?'

'I am prepared to apologise. Jane said she was with you. You said you were here. It was the obvious thing to think.'

'Thanks very much, Nick.'

'All right, Alan. Maybe I should have known you better.'

'Yes. You should.'

'Jane told Miss Cotterel she was with you.'

'Then Jane's a . . .'

Nick sat on the arm of the chair. He stared at the wild

trees tossing in the rain outside.

'Is she? Is Jane a liar?'

'No. She's not.'

'No, she's not,' Nick repeated softly. 'Jane's not a liar. She's a nice girl. A nice girl who deliberately fabricated a story. Why?'

'I don't know.'

'Nor do I.'

'Maybe Jimmy does.'

'Jimmy? Was he with you too?'

'No. He wasn't with us. It was something Jane said. She said Jimmy knew.'

'What does Jimmy know?'

'Don't ask daft questions. If I knew I'd tell you. Ask him. The girl must have gone mad.'

'Which brings me to another point,' Nick said. 'Mad! That wasn't the only reason Miss Cotterel was mad. Apparently she doesn't like Jane being out at night. She told us she'd locked Jane in her bedroom and that someone had let her out. She seemed to think it was you who let Jane out.'

'Yes.'

'Is that all you can say?'

'Yes. But it's not a bedroom, Nick. She locks her in the flipping laboratory. Down the garden. Bolts and shutters, like a gaol. She wanted to come to the dance so we let her out.'

'We?'

'I.'

'Mmm. And what business is it of yours? What right have you got to go trespassing on Miss Cotterel's property? She's given Jane a good home. She's clothed and fed her. She's better looked after now than she ever was with her grandmother. If Miss Cotterel believes that

92

Jane is better locked in at night then who are you to think otherwise? You let Jane out and what happened? The girl disappeared into the night until after four. If that's the sort of thing Jane does then I think the lady is sensible to lock her in.'

'I didn't know the daft coot was going to do that. How was I to know? I didn't think there was any harm in taking her to a dance.'

'So you didn't think? Well it's time you did think. If you set one foot on Miss Cotterel's property again she's going to the police.'

'She can't do that.'

'She can. The Englishman protects his castle.'

'I haven't done anything.'

'Alan, you've done more than enough.'

'It's an injustice.'

'Is it?'

'You know it is.'

'I know one thing . . . she means what she says. You stay away from El Garda, and you stay away from Jane.'

'That's not fair.'

'Have I to spell it out for you? Stay away from Jane. *Right* away. D'you hear?'

'I hear. You can't make me.'

'For once you'll do as you're told.'

'And if I don't?'

'I wear a belt with a metal buckle,' Nick said. 'I shall use it.'

Alan stared at him. 'You mean it, don't you?'

'I mean it. I'll go and see the lady after dinner and explain that Jane was not with you last night. I doubt if she'll believe me, but I'll do my best to scrape some of the mud off your reputation.'

'Don't bother. I'll tell the old bag myself.'

'Oh no you won't. You set neither foot nor finger in that place. And just one more thing.'

'What?'

'You might tell your friend James that the same will apply to him.'

'What's Jimmy done?'

'Nothing. It's what he might do. Take Jane to another dance. Just tell him not to.'

'I'll tell him,' Alan muttered.

I'll wring his blinking neck. It was his idea. Jane, you idiot. What have you said? And what does Jimmy know about you?

I T was May. The curls of green bracken were beginning to uncurl. Coltsfoot grew between the railway sleepers and daisies on the side. Grasses were becoming tall and feathery, and larches were vivid with new leaves. The oaks too, all over the hills, bursting with greeny-yellow buds.

If the oak before the ash we shall only have a splash.

An ash. Alan stared at the trees. Which was an ash? The leafless one down there by the pond? Could be. Could be a nice, hot summer. He picked up a stone. The pond was a long way off, about a quarter of a mile. Alan missed it.

'Watch where you're bunging them stones,' someone said. 'Oh, it's you.'

Jimmy scrambled up the embankment out of the thicket of witch hazel.

'Good afternoon, James. How's your cold?' Jimmy had spent a fortnight in bed.

'Bronchitis,' Jimmy said. 'Not a cold.'

'Nasty,' Alan remarked. 'Are you going anywhere in particular?'

Jimmy leant on his gun.

'Rabbiting. You coming?'

'So long as it's not all the way to Langdon Point.'

They went together down the railway line, following the rust-red rails as far as the bridge. Their feet sent up puffs of dry dust to powder their shoes. A cuckoo called from a telegraph pole, jackdaws cawed behind the hills, traffic speeded beneath them, sounding hollow. Alan hung over the bridge and looked down.

'We've been here six months. It seems like years. Nothing ever changes here, does it?'

'Not much,' Jimmy said. 'Beats me why you came. Daft! Nick working in London and you moving down here. Daft!'

There was a pause which the cuckoo filled.

'If you must know, my mother had a nervous breakdown. Nick thought it would be better for her to live in the country.'

'Down here? All this way? What about the South Downs? Kent? That's country. The New Forest? Winchester? What about there? Daft coming right down here.'

'Have you any idea of the price of property around Winchester? Nick's not a millionaire. We picked up Amberley House cheap. Not that it's any of your business anyway.'

'Me Mam,' Jimmy said, 'likes to know everything. It worries her, not knowing. Why can't Nick get a job in Hasley General?'

Jimmy's mother was a nosy old bag.

'Maybe Nick doesn't *want* a job in Hasley General.'

'Not high class enough, I suppose? Not enough private patients?'

'Nick's not that sort of doctor.'

'National Health Service not his line?'

'He qualified,' Alan explained, 'then he took up another branch of medicine. He's been doing research for years. Antibiotics and that sort of thing. He reckons they'll be able to cure cancer in another five years.'

'That so? Hark at that cuckoo.' Jimmy aimed the gun at the telegraph pole.

'You're not going to shoot it?'

'Waste a bullet on a flipping cuckoo? I was just

96

getting my eye in. Pow! Right through the head. He's dead. Intestines hanging on the wires.' The cuckoo went silent, then streaked across the sky to the trees. Alan picked up a stone. Aimed it at a cat's eye down on the road. Missed. Watched it bounce. Once, twice, five times into the gully at the side.

'It's better doing it on water,' Jimmy said. 'I used to be able to skim them right across the pond.'

Alan climbed through the fence on the other side of the bridge. Jimmy followed.

'Where are we going?'

'Anywhere,' Alan said.

The path was almost vertical in places. It wound between rocks and clumps of golden gorse right to the top. The climb was steep, slippery where the grass was worn away, exposing patches of damp red soil. Jimmy sweated with the sun on his back. His chest was beginning to feel tight again. Heaving to catch air. He could hear his own breathing. He reached the trees and flung himself down on the grass. Langdon Woods were over him. He was weak like an old man. Shouldn't have come out. Mam said not to go out yet.

'Are you all right?' Alan asked.

'Aye,' Jimmy wheezed.

'You look ill.'

'I need a couple of Bob Martins. I must be out of condition.'

Alan sat on a stone and chewed a grass.

'I've been wanting a few words with you.'

Jimmy's breathing grew easier.

'What about?'

'Jane.'

'Oh her,' Jimmy said.

'I suppose you heard?'

'Heard?'

97

'About me and Jane.'

Jimmy looked up. His lank hair was sticking to his forehead.

'What about you and Jane?'

'Didn't your mother tell you? The Lydcroft grapevine must have slipped up. I thought your mother knew everything.'

'Me Mam hates gossip. What about you and Jane?'

'That night we took her to the dance she got back at ten past four in the morning. The legend states she spent the night with me.'

Jimmy raised an eyebrow, then laughed.

'That's a good one. Who made that up?'

'Jane did.'

'Jane said that?'

'Yes.'

'*Jane* said it?'

'It wasn't true,' Alan said hastily.

'I know that,' Jimmy said. 'I saw her.'

'When?'

'That night.'

'You saw Jane? When? What time?'

''Bout . . . let me think. One-thirty? It was just gone one when Potter and me left Hasley. Half an hour to Green Bottom. He dropped me off and I walked up. Just after one-thirty I'd say. Quarter to two maybe. She was standing on top of Winnard's Leap with the dog.'

'You couldn't have.'

'I did.'

'It was dark. You couldn't have seen her.'

'It was moonlight, boy. Bright moonlight. She was right against the skyline. I happened to look up and there she was, Brainy Bates with her piled-up hair. I was going to shout, but she was gone next time I looked.'

'You're quite sure?'

98

'I saw her.'

'There was a hell of a row,' Alan said. 'Fanny Cotterel threatened to get the police. Jane had said she was with me and the old bat believed her; so did Nick until I denied it. What was she doing on top of Winnard's Leap? What was she doing out until four o'clock in the morning?'

'Haven't you asked her?'

'She's avoided me, and Miss Cotterel has taken to driving her to school and back.'

'Don't you know what she was doing?' Jimmy asked.

'No. Do you?'

'She was watching the stars, man. That's what she was doing. Watching the stars.'

The air was warm, and heavy with bees humming over the gorse flowers. Jane had said something about the stars. Something significant. He almost knew but it slipped away. He could ask her but Nick had put his foot down. He hadn't to speak to Jane. It was a rotten injustice.

'Jimmy?' Alan said.

'Hello.' Jimmy was lying on his back staring up through the trees to the sky.

'Would you do me a favour?'

'Depends what it is.'

'Tell Fanny Cotterel you saw Jane that night and she wasn't with me.'

'Tell her yourself.'

'I can't. I'm not allowed near the place or Jane. She wouldn't listen to me anyway.'

'You can't expect me to walk in there unarmed and defenceless.'

'You've got the gun. She'll listen to you, Jim. She's got no reason not to.'

'I'll be mashed to pulp. I let Jane out.'

'I got the blame for that.'

'Didn't you tell her it was me?'

'Why should I? It wouldn't have made any difference.'

Jimmy sat up.

'I was going rabbiting.'

'Jimmy, please.'

'I've to take things easy for a couple of weeks. If I get upset I might have a relapse.'

'Jaundice is a nasty illness,' Alan said.

'Jaundice?'

'It leaves you yellow.'

'Funny boy. OK. Let's go.'

Jimmy skidded down to the railway and under the wire.

'You'll do it?'

'Aye.'

Jimmy jammed his finger on the door bell. The chimes sounded loud inside.

'You can't blow something up just by looking at it,' Alan said.

'You can burn a piece of paper by holding a magnifying glass between it and the sun. You don't touch it with the flame but it'll still burn.'

'That's elementary physics. Heat magnified. Concentrated on one spot.'

'Jane works the same way. Concentrate enough power on one spot and it will explode.'

Jimmy rang the bell again. Bees hummed over purple lilac. Hot scented silence surged back.

'Jane's a human being,' Alan said. 'Not a ray gun or a convex lens.'

Jimmy shrugged.

'You asked me and I told you. It fits; like fractions. Jane's the common denominator. The one thing that was there each time. The one thing that links the juke-box, your washing machine and Granny Bates' telly.'

'But it's power, Jimmy. Where does she get the power?'

Jimmy looked up. 'The stars are powerful,' he said.

'What a load of codswollop. They must be out.'

Jimmy tried the door. It opened.

'You're not going in?'

'Why not?'

'You can't. It's someone's house. You can't just walk in.'

'I can. That old bat knows. That's why she locks Jane in. To keep her away from the stars.'

The refrigerator was humming in the kitchen.

'Come out,' Alan said. 'If they've left the door open they can't be far away.'

'Hang on a minute. What's in here? The living-room. What a mess.'

Jimmy walked along the hall opening the doors.

'Spare bedroom. She could have put Jane in here. No shutters though. This must be *her* bedroom.'

'Let's go,' Alan said impatiently.

'What's in here?' Jimmy asked.

It was a room at the back. Through the window Jimmy could see the garden, the laboratory, the hills rearing behind. The dour face of Elgin.

'Looks like the physics lab,' Jimmy said.

There was a bench with a bunsen burner. A glass-fronted cupboard containing a microscope, rows of test tubes and bottles of chemicals.

'She's converted it,' Jimmy said. 'Leonard's left-overs.'

'For God's sake let's get out.'

'What's that on the table?'

'An empty jam jar.'

Jimmy crossed the room. 'It's not empty.'

Alan joined him. Knelt on the floor to skyline the jar. It was not empty. It was full of sun. Inside was a small cloud of mist: floating, drifting. Moving under its own motivation. Changing shape, expanding, coming together again. A dance of microscopic particles. A smoky kaleidoscope. Each particle split the sunlight into prisms of colour. It was a dancing rainbow, gone before he really saw it. Reappearing. Its effect was hypnotic.

'What is it?' Jimmy asked.

'It's fascinating.'

'But what is it? Gas?'

'Could be.'

'What's it in there for?'

'How would I know?'

'You can't see gas,' Jimmy said.

'You wouldn't if it wasn't for the sun. You don't see dust in the air until the particles get caught up in a sunbeam. Then you see them moving.'

'Dust then? Moving.'

'It's not dust,' Alan said. 'Watch it. It's not just moving anywhere. Watch it.'

It went in a spiral to the top of the jar. Hovered under the lid. Fell to the bottom again where it collected in a ball like a great shining marble. Then broke, crept up the side, hugging close to the glass.

'Trying to find a way out,' Jimmy said.

Alan dragged his eyes away. 'And that's what we ought to be doing.'

He glanced along a row of dull bound science books. Cell structure. Anatomy of bats. Hypersensitivity. Miss Cotterel must be pretty brainy to understand those.

There was a key in the cupboard door. Jimmy unlocked it and reached the microscope. He stood it on the bench next to a rack of glass slides.

'We'll get caught in here if you don't come on,' Alan said.

Jimmy waved his hand and moved a slide under the eye-piece.

'I've always wanted to try one of these. Hello!'

'Goodbye.'

'Don't go. Look at this.'

Jimmy moved over. Picked up the slide. Held it to the light.

'It looks like dried blood,' Jimmy said. 'But it moved. Blood doesn't move, does it?'

'Let's have a look.'

Jimmy put the slide back under the microscope. Alan peered through. He could see nothing but grey. He twiddled the focus knob. The grey split into shapes, became clearer. Grey shapes with darker centres. Cytoplasm and nucleii. Single cells with thread-like tendrils. They were moving.

'That's odd,' Alan said. 'They don't look like amoebae. Pity Nick's not here. He'd know. And I'm going.'

'Lead on,' Jimmy said. Alan disappeared. Jimmy slipped the small glass slides into his pocket. He had a feeling that it was important. What were those small moving things? Nick would know. He went into the scented garden, along the path and shut the gate. El Garda above the door.

'Phew!' Alan said as they went up the path. 'I was sweating with fear.'

Jimmy stopped, bent over something beside the path. A stone had been rolled away, exposing the earth underneath and a heap of whitened bones.

'Rabbit bones,' Jimmy said. 'She found it then.'

'Who found it?'

'Jane. She found the rabbit.'

Jimmy glanced round the silent hills. It so very nearly fitted. Stars and rabbits. They went together somehow.

103

But how? Stars and rabbits. A breath of wind came suddenly cold, reminding him of winter, the dark nights and the stars, and late frost which nipped the blossoms of the fruit trees. The wind was breathing, something walking soft-footed behind him. An intelligence invisible in the air. Jimmy turned round. Jane, in her scarlet dress, was standing outside the Battery House watching them.

Jimmy hauled himself over the last ridge. Old stone walls were built into the hillside, making a kind of room, and other walls, only a few stones high and covered in places with brambles and rank grass, showed where other rooms had been. He could smell sheep. A hundred years ago it had been an iron-ore factory. He could hear the gurgle of water coming from nearby. The spring which came from the hill and went by pipes under the road and railway to fill the pond. He could see the track where the carts had gone. Over the other side of the road, embracing the railway, was wild open country: Lydcroft Common, bracken, gorse, and plantations of larches. Beyond that was Bowler's Tump, houses small and hazy in the distance. The place hadn't changed much in a hundred years except to fall to ruin.

'I've been in bed a fortnight,' Jimmy said.

'I thought I hadn't seen you at school,' Jane said.

'Bronchitis. I won't be there next week either. Have to get acclimatized gradually. This is the first time I've been out.'

'You don't look ill.'

'Well, I'm better, aren't I? Almost. Where've you been this afternoon? We called in and you were out.'

'I wasn't. I was in my bedroom. I saw you go out. We went out earlier on. To the May Pool in the car. Marcia had to go into Langdon to do some shopping, so she dropped me off at the bottom of the path on the way back.'

Alan sat silent on a stone some little distance away. Keep away from Jane, Nick had said. He didn't know what to say to her.

'You've been out in the car then?' Jimmy asked her.

'Yes. The bluebells are just coming out.'

'I thought you were scared of cars.' Jimmy was not looking at Jane. He was watching the cloud shadows drifting in light and shade across the common. Alan saw her clench her fist.

'I'm not scared of cars,' Jane said.

'Oh. I thought you were.'

'I'm not.'

Jimmy put a grass between his teeth and stared pensively. His hair fell forward and covered his eyes. The gun lay gleaming by his feet.

'I always thought you had a memory like an elephant. But you haven't. You'll never pass them exams if you keep forgetting things.'

'I don't forget.'

'When did Queen Victoria come to the throne?'

Jane looked surprised.

'Nineteen hundred and one, I think. Why?'

'That was when she came *off* the throne.'

'Oh yes. Eighteen thirty-six then. Right?'

'I haven't the foggiest. How's your piano playing going?'

'I haven't played for ages. Not since that day . . .' Jane stopped. 'I can't play the piano,' she said.

'You just said you could.'

'I didn't.'

'You just said it, girl.'

'I can't play the piano. You know I can't.'

'I don't know anything,' Jimmy said.

105

'You do.'

'All right. I know everything so you'd better confess.'

'I don't know what you're talking about, Jimmy.'

'I don't know what you're talking about,' Jimmy repeated in a high-pitched voice. 'How about stars?'

'Stars?' Jane's grey eyes were wide, but her hands were still clenched at her sides. White at the knuckles.

'Stars,' Jimmy said. 'The twinkle sort. Power. Electric voltage. I want to know how you do it.'

'What is this place?' Alan asked loudly.

'An iron-ore factory,' Jane said. 'How do I do what?'

'Use the stars to blow up machines.'

The tension was building up.

'I don't do that.'

'You do. I told you I know everything.'

'You're stupid.'

'You're dangerous.'

'You've been in the B class all the way up through school. You don't know anything.'

Alan had to break the tension before something snapped.

'Why did they build an iron-ore factory up here?' Alan asked.

'Romans,' Jimmy said.

Jane crept away, towards the break in the wall where the door used to be and the path went up over the top of Winnard's Leap.

'The Romans built it,' Jimmy said. 'Then someone else built it again on the same site. Come here, Bates! I haven't finished yet.'

Jane hesitated, then came back.

'Why did you tell Fanny Cotterel you were with Alan till four o'clock in the morning? I saw you. You weren't with him at all. You were on your own, standing on top of Winnard's Leap watching the flipping stars.'

'Don't keep on at her,' Alan said. 'You've said enough.'

'I saw you,' Jimmy said. 'With my own two eyes. I spy. Alan wasn't with you, Jane Bates. Why did you say he was?'

'Forget it, can't you?' Alan said. 'It's history now.'

'You keep out of it. It's her I'm talking to, not you. What were you doing up there, Janie? Charging up your batteries with star power? What are you going to blow up next? Old Cobbler's computer? Alan's car? Fanny Cotterel's fridge?'

'No!' Jane said.

'I want to know how you do it.'

'Leave off, Jimmy. You don't know what you're on about. If you stopped to think you'd know it was impossible. Nick said it was impossible. You've got stars on your brain.'

'Is it?' Jimmy demanded. 'Is it impossible? Tell him, Jane. Go on. Tell him.'

There was a bird piping down by the pond. The same sad notes over and over again.

'Let's have it. Let's have it all. Right from the rabbit.'

Jane's hands were tightly clenched. Alan could see blood seeping through her fingers where her nails had broken the skin. She took one step backwards.

'She's had enough,' Alan said.

'Enough? She hasn't started yet. Come on, Bates. Start talking.'

'No!' Her voice was choked. Her face was white. Her eyes huge and staring. She was fighting, struggling and she didn't know why. Jimmy wouldn't stop. He went on and he wouldn't stop. Something was so tight inside her she felt she would snap. She took another step back.

'Stay right where you are, Jane Bates.'

'Leave her alone.'

'Not yet, boy. You're not backing out this time, girl.

Come on. Talk!'

Jane turned and fled, a flash of red through the bracken. They watched her to the top of the rise then the path dipped and she was gone. Jimmy sat on the wall.

'Damn, damn, damn. What's she run off for, the idiot?'

'I told you to leave her alone. I could see she couldn't take any more.'

'Haven't you any idea what I was doing?'

'Apart from being an insufferable bore, no.'

'Didn't you see? Didn't you see the way she tensed up? The way she reacted? Didn't it occur to you to wonder why? I wanted her to break. A few more minutes and she'd have broken. She knows. Down inside she knows everything. A few more minutes and she'd have told. If you'd kept your great mouth shut she'd have told everything.'

Alan stared at the summer shining hills. They were empty. No movement anywhere. 'If you want to know what I think: I think you're a louse. You kept on and on at her. You say you wanted her to talk but you didn't give her a chance.'

The bird was still piping down by the pond and a plane somewhere was coming nearer. Jimmy stared up at the sky. The noise tore the silence. Shattered it completely.

'A chance?' Jimmy shouted. 'Give her a flaming chance and she'd blow up half the world. I tell you she doesn't know what she's doing, let alone remember what she's done. It's not a conscious action. It's a reflex action. Automatic. You're scared of moths so what do you do? Squash them, then there's nothing left to be scared of. That's what Jane does. A quick swat and it's gone. Not moths, though. Machines. Any machines. That thing up there.'

Jimmy aimed his gun at the plane. It passed overhead, dived down to the horizon trailing its screaming noise behind it. He kept it in line with his gun barrel: a silver shining machine. Jane would hate it. Hate its noise. Its noise drove away thought. If he pulled the trigger he wouldn't hear the bang. The plane's engines would drown the bang. Drown Jane's bang too . . . drown her deadly silent power.

'And there's a great deal of difference between swatting a moth and blowing up an aeroplane,' Alan shouted back.

Jimmy saw a flash, brief and bright, low in the sky, sun on silver, or a barb of lightning. The noise of the plane stopped suddenly and suddenly Alan's voice was very loud: a great deal of difference between swatting a moth and blowing up an aeroplane. In the silence that came Jimmy watched a faint drift of smoke, or was it a grey drift of cloud, melting away. Then the sky was pure blue and utterly still.

He turned. His eyes raked the green bracken hills behind him. Nothing there. No one there. Not Jane. But the hills could hide her, the dips, the hollows, the rocks. She could be watching the sky from the top of Winnard's Leap and the hills would hide her. There was summer all around, bright yellow summer sun and it shone cold. It turned his sweat shivering cold. The sky where the plane had gone was cold too. High and cold.

'No!' Jimmy whispered.

'Yes, there is,' Alan said. 'They're so different you can't make a comparison like that.'

'She wouldn't,' Jimmy said. 'She wouldn't do that, would she?'

'Now what are you talking about?'

Jimmy's mouth was dry. He glanced round. Alan's dark eyes met his own.

'That plane,' Jimmy said. 'Jane wouldn't blow up that,

would she? There were men in it. Men. They'd be dead. She'd think of that. Surely she'd think of that. Of the men inside.'

'You mug! It's gone over the horizon.'

Jimmy pounded the gun against the ground.

'Has it?'

'Of course it has. It'll be over the Irish Sea by now.'

'I didn't see it. I was watching it all the time but I didn't see it go over the horizon. I didn't see it go. I saw a flash over the trees. And the noise. The noise stopped suddenly. It didn't peter out. It just stopped.'

'Give me patience,' Alan muttered. 'If I were you, Jimmy, I should get back to bed. There's something seriously wrong with you. You're delirious.'

Jimmy stood up. He could see the tops of the trees above Winnard's Leap.

'She's up there somewhere. She hasn't had time to get home. She was strung up. She could have done it. Jane could have done it, Alan.'

'I don't believe you,' Alan said quietly.

A cuckoo started calling. Jimmy's teeth were chattering. He couldn't stop shivering. He tucked his gun under his arm. He ought to go home.

'You'll believe me one day, boyo. I only hope it won't be too late: when they're singing funeral hymns around your grave. Exploded and laid to rest. I'm going home. I don't feel too good.'

'I should,' Alan said. 'I find you pretty sickening.'

The newsreader spoke impersonally.

'A military aircraft exploded in mid-air this afternoon near Newport in Monmouthshire. The plane was making its third trial run. The crew of five were killed and wreckage was strewn over a wide area. A tractor driver and two other agricultural workers were taken to hospital with facial injuries. The cause of the explosion is not yet known. Air Ministry officials are to begin a full investigation.

'In London today armed men broke into a clearing bank . . .'

Alan switched off the television. It left him cold. Everything Jimmy had said came rushing back. But it couldn't have been Jane. She had been miles away. Out on the hills near him and Jimmy. It couldn't have been Jane.

'I T' s a lovely day,' Alan said.

'Yes,' said Jane.

'Are you doing anything in particular?'

'No.'

'Not taking Marcia and the pugs on a nature trail?'

'Marcia's turning out the attic.'

The sign of a miner creaked outside Green Bottom public house. Above was a haze of bluebells in Langdon Woods. Alan could smell them, bluebells mixed with beer. Under the bridge was a dark pool of shadow, but everywhere else sunlight, and a warm breeze which rustled the crisp-packets people had thrown down. Alan pocketed his mother's packet of cigarettes, and glanced towards the Battery House. The windows stared back black and empty.

'I haven't had a chance to talk to you,' Alan said. 'Will you come out for a drive?'

'Now?'

'I'll have to fetch the car.'

'Now?'

'Say half an hour.'

Jane glanced up the path. Her pale brown hair hung loose and gold with sun. 'She won't let me. Not with you.'

'Don't tell her. We'll go for the day. The Welsh mountains. Brecon Beacons. You needn't say you're going with me. Say you're going with someone else.'

'Who?'

'I don't know. Haven't you any friends?'

'There's Caroline.'

'Caroline Hunt?'

'I could tell Marcia I was going to spend the day with her.'

'And you'll tell Marcia that? You'll come?'

'Yes.'

'Good girl. Half an hour. Walk up to the common and I'll pick you up. No one will see. Half an hour then.'

'Yes,' Jane said.

A car rushed by with a smell of petrol. Heat shimmered on the surface of the road. Jimmy said Jane was petrified of machines.

'If you don't want to come in the car we could go for a walk.'

She looked puzzled.

'If you don't like cars and you'd rather not come, I don't mind. We can go for a walk.'

'What a funny thing to say. Anyone would think I was scared of cars. They're just machines. Why should I mind them?'

Machines? They were far away, out of her thoughts, out of her mind. The world was bright with sun and flowers. The smell of petrol had gone. Jane laughed.

'Then you'll come in the car?' Alan asked.

'Of course!'

He smiled.

'Half an hour then. I'll see you, Jane.'

Alan pulled in on the edge of the common and opened the door.

'Been waiting long?'

'I've only just got here.'

Jane slid inside. The white pug followed her and settled himself on the floor by her feet. Alan felt irritated. Why bring the flipping dog?

'I couldn't leave him behind,' Jane said. 'I always take him with me. I couldn't leave him.'

Alan forced his irritation away.

'She let you come then?'

'I told her I was going to Caroline's for the day. She didn't say anything except that she'd fetch me at nine, so we'll have to be back at about quarter to.'

Alan glanced at his watch.

'That gives us nearly ten hours. All day, Jane. Just you and me. Phew! It's like an oven in here. I'll take the roof off. It won't take a minute. If you want an apple help yourself. There's a bagful in the front.'

Jane took a bite. It was bright yellow and tasted of sun. There was mould round the pips. Alan undid the screws and lifted the roof off. He spread the canvas on the grass and folded it. Jane felt the sun striking hot on her back and heard the gorse-pods popping. A grasshopper whirring. It was going to be a perfect day.

'Did you tell your mother you were taking me out?' Jane asked.

Alan opened the boot.

'No. I told her I was taking Jimmy out. To Brecon Beacons. Jimmy would like that. He really appreciates the wide open spaces.'

Jane spluttered.

'Jimmy wouldn't go to the mountains if you dragged him. His great ambition is to own a garage in London.'

Alan stowed away the framework and canvas.

'Mum doesn't know that. If it had been Nick I'd have said something different. Nick's shrewd. But he's staying in London this weekend. He's reached the climax of an important experiment with his bugs and can't leave them.'

'Bugs?' said Jane. 'Germs you mean?'

Alan sat beside her.

'Antibiotics,' Alan explained. 'This latest culture they've been working on has apparently cured cancer in rats. Nick rang up last night. You'd have thought he'd discovered gold instead of a few microscopic bugs.'

He switched on the ignition. The engine came with a gentle purr. He put his foot on the accelerator. The revs grew louder. He was watching Jane. Her hands clasped loosely in her lap, her placid eyes staring over the summer country. Who said she was afraid of machines? Alan slid the car into gear. Winston whined.

'All right?' Alan asked Jane.

She smiled, picked up the dog and held him close.

'Fine.'

'Off we go then.'

The car moved from the grass to the road. Overhead an aeroplane droned. Alan glanced up as he swung round towards Bowler's Tump and Langdon.

'That aeroplane crash was a terrible thing,' Alan said. 'Five men killed. Did you know it was the one me and Jimmy were watching that afternoon?'

Jane's grey eyes clouded.

'Not you too? Not you as well as Jimmy?'

Alan touched her hand.

'Forget it, girl.'

He gave a loud blast on the horn and waved.

'Who was that?' Jane asked.

'The devil,' Alan said. 'Jimmy himself.'

Jimmy had met Mrs Mackenzie. She was walking down to catch the twenty past eleven bus from Lydcroft Common. Jimmy wondered why she seemed so surprised to see him until he learnt that he was supposed to be on his way to the Brecon Beacons with Alan. Jimmy couldn't think what to say. He'd just seen Alan off with Jane. Of course. Nick had put his foot down. Jimmy muttered something about remembering he had to play cricket that afternoon so Alan had dropped him off just up the road. Then he remembered Alan had borrowed his cricket bat and hadn't returned it. He was obliged to ask for it. The bus came rumbling up the hill. Alan's mother thrust a key in his hand, told him the bat was in the hall-stand, to go and get it.

Put the key under the mat when you come out.

Jimmy opened the gate of Amberley House. He didn't want the blessed bat. He'd have to get it though, else she'd know there was something funny going on. Why should he have to cover up for Alan and Jane? Flipping mountains! Who wanted to go there? He let himself into the kitchen.

After the brilliance of the sunlight outside, the hall seemed gloomy. Jimmy found the bat amongst umbrellas and walking sticks. The silence echoed every move he made. He turned thankfully to go. Right beside him the telephone started ringing. Jimmy jumped. He ignored it as far as the kitchen but its noise was insistent. He went back and lifted the receiver.

'Hello. Langdon 269.'

'Alan? Listen. I've got to get hold of Jimmy. Can you find him, bring him to the 'phone and ring me back? I'm at the hospital. Get a pen and write down the number.'

Jimmy was startled into silence.

'Alan? Are you still there? Write down the number then find Jimmy quickly. It's LON/ . . . Alan?'

'I'm not Alan,' Jimmy said. 'I *am* Jimmy. Is that you, Nick? What do you want me for?'

'Jimmy! Thank goodness. Listen, that slide you gave me a couple of weeks ago; where did you get it?'

Jimmy shifted his feet.

'I can't tell you that.'

'Jimmy, I have to know.'

116

'It could land me in gaol. I pinched it.'

'Where from?'

'Miss Cotterel's.'

'Damn! I was hoping you wouldn't say that.'

'Why? What is it?'

There was silence.

'Is that all you wanted to know?' Jimmy asked.

Still silence.

'Nick?'

'Don't go away, Jimmy. You remember that theory you had about Jane blowing things up . . .'

'The one you said was stupid?'

'Yes. That one. I hate to say it but I think you're probably right.'

Jimmy felt cold all over.

'Jim?' Nick said. 'Are you still there?'

'You can't say that,' Jimmy said. 'When I said it, it didn't matter because everyone said I didn't know what I was on about. It can't be true. How do you know?'

'Because of that slide.'

'Oh, that.'

'Yes. That. It could cause the biggest sensation since the Americans landed on the moon.'

'But that mightn't be anything to do with Jane. It might be one of the old bat's experiments. There were loads of test tubes and bunsen burners in there.'

'I am very much afraid it has everything to do with Jane,' Nick said. 'Do you want to know? It was your idea originally. Do you want to know how right you were?'

The hallway was chilly. Sunlight filtered through the coloured glass of the front door. Jimmy's hands were icy cold.

'It's rather horrible,' Nick said.

'I'll take it,' Jimmy said.

'OK then. You can have it on the understanding that you keep it to yourself. You can tell Anna and Alan but certainly not Jane, although she may already know because Miss Cotterel knows. But you'd better say nothing to Jane, Jimmy.'

'What were those things?' Jimmy asked. 'They were moving when I saw them.'

'They were still moving. They are still moving now. They are nerve cells. Neurons.'

Jimmy was surprised. He had been expecting something horrible.

'Is that all?'

'Neurons, Jimmy.'

'I heard what you said.'

'Have you ever seen nerve cells move on their own?'

Jimmy paused. The human brain was made up of nerve cells.

'No,' Jimmy said.

'Nor have I,' Nick said. 'Nor has anyone else. Nerve cells are part of higher animals. These are self-supporting, and self-motivating. We think they are a form of protozoa.'

'Protowhat?'

'Protozoa. Single-celled organisms.'

'Oh. I see.'

'Do you?' Nick asked. 'How much do you know about protozoa?'

Jimmy considered.

'Nothing,' he admitted.

'They are like any other animal or plant. They need certain substances in order to live. Oxygen or nitrogen, water, minerals, suitable temperature and food, either from external sources or from photosynthesis in the case of plants. These things can remain alive in a vacuum, in boiling water or in cold well below zero.

118

They're dormant under these conditions but they are alive. It appears the only thing they need in order to live is starlight.'

'That's significant,' Jimmy said. 'It's odd, too.'

'Do you want me to go on?'

'Yes.'

'When you gave me that slide I didn't think it was important. I gave it to a colleague of mine to play around with. He's been studying it for two weeks. Of course Vic Watson only had a few cells to work with and he could be wrong, but he thinks they have some intelligence.'

'Intelligence?'

'It's hard to explain. One cell on its own is useless, but in some way they can communicate with each other. Together they make a body with co-ordinated movements. It's almost like a brain which can disintegrate and come together again. Together they have a purpose.'

'That sounds nasty.'

'I haven't finished yet. Vic has tested them with stimuli. There was no reaction to temperature changes, light intensity, smell or sound. They have a slight sense of touch but being pricked with a pin doesn't worry them. The only thing which has any effect on them is machines. They're petrified of them. Vic discovered it quite by chance. He put them on top of the fridge. They must have felt the vibrations.'

'Jane's scared of machines,' Jimmy said.

'Yes,' said Nick. 'So you once said.'

'It doesn't fit, though,' Jimmy said. 'She's not just scared of machines. She blows them up. How's *she* blow them up? How *does* she collect the power?'

'These little cells use starlight as their source of energy, Jimmy. And that's not all. They can also transmit this energy in the form of highly intense cosmic rays. When Vic put them on the fridge they blasted cosmic radiation until their energy was exhausted. After that they remained dormant. He even thought they were dead until he put them in direct starlight and they were able to produce more energy. Now does it fit?'

'Oh God!' Jimmy said. 'So that's it. That's how Jane does it. It's not her at all. It's those things. She's got those things inside her.'

'It would seem so,' Nick agreed.

'How? How did they get there?'

'They can't travel through solid matter,' Nick said. 'If they are inside Jane then they must have gained entry through an open wound.'

'Like some disease,' Jimmy said. 'Some horrible disease. Out of that flaming rabbit. It bit her. Out of the rabbit, Nick. Rabbits have little things inside their intestines, don't they?'

'They do, but the bacteria in the caecum of a rabbit are nothing like these. These *could* have been in the rabbit and passed to Jane when it bit her. I don't know for sure.'

'Where on earth did they come from in the first place?'

'Not Earth,' Nick said.

'Eh?'

'They're of extra-terrestrial origin.'

'Give over.'

'They're not from this Earth, Jimmy. We've never seen anything like them.'

'Pull the other one.'

'Protozoa with intelligence? Nerve cells that are self-supporting? I'm not joking. There's not a living cell on Earth that resembles them.'

'You're telling me they come from outer space?'

'Well, they can't be from this solar system,' Nick said. 'Or they'd utilise sunlight instead of starlight. They get their energy from starlight at night, when galactic radiation is more intense than solar radiation. They're probably from within our own galaxy. Light from another galaxy would be too weak to provide sufficient energy. Rigel, Betelgeux, a blue star maybe with different combination of elements from those of our own sun. God only knows where they're from.'

'You mean it?'

'Yes. I mean it.'

'It's horrible.'

'Yes.'

'Things from space inside Jane. They're in Jane. Things from space. It's horrible. What are you going to do?'

'I don't know.'

'You've got to do something.'

'Something, but what? Miss Cotterel must have studied them, too. She probably knows more than I do. She has the right idea. Keep Jane away from the starlight and the cells remain dormant. Without energy, without power.'

'And we let her out,' Jimmy muttered. 'We let her see the stars. Why didn't the stupid woman say something?'

'She's done all she can, Jimmy. But it's not enough. I'll come down and talk to her. I only hope Jane's own instinct, or rather the instinct of those cells, will keep her away from machines. I'll come down tomorrow.'

Jimmy shifted uneasily. To blab, or not to blab? That was the question.

'Nick,' Jimmy said. 'Jane herself isn't afraid of machines. They used all their power to blow up that plane.'

'That's surmise, Jimmy. We don't *know* that. We don't *know*.'

'That's a commonsense guess. One and one makes two. She did it. Their power's gone and Jane's not afraid any more. She's gone out with Alan in his car. They've gone for the day.'

121

Jimmy heard something drop at the other end.

'I told Alan to keep away from her,' Nick said angrily.

'He won't thank me for telling you.'

'I'll wring his confounded neck. Why can't he do what he's told?'

'Maybe he doesn't like being told.'

'Never mind what he likes. Where's he gone? D'you know?'

'The Welsh mountains.'

'Oh hell! I can't phone him there, can I? I can't understand why the woman let Jane go with him. You'd think she'd have more sense. Tell Alan to ring me when he gets back, will you?'

'He's gone. I can't tell him if he's gone.'

'Leave a message then!' Nick sounded irritated.

'What's the number?' Jimmy asked.

'My flat after eight. He knows the number. Where's Anna?'

'She's out.'

'Then . . .'

'I just came to get my bat,' Jimmy said. 'I'm going now. She said to put the key under the mat. I'll leave a message. Cheerio.'

Jimmy dropped the phone.

Hell fire and damnation! If that twerp had believed what he'd said he wouldn't be belting round the country with a load of dynamite in his car. First sight of stars and his car would go sky high. She'd blow it up. Jimmy shrugged. That wasn't his business, was it? Brought it on himself, hadn't he? He didn't even like Alan particularly. His innards would be splattered all over the road. Jimmy locked the door and put the key under the mat. He could try hitching. Get walking, Jimmy boy! It's a long way to Brecon.

13

T H E Y were called the Brecon Beacons so they wouldn't
have gone to Brynmawr. Alan wouldn't know you could
get to them from Brynmawr. He'd have gone straight to
Brecon and followed the signposts: to the mountain
centre. Jimmy kept his eyes skinned all along the road.
There was only one way signposted: to the mountain
centre. The sign had said four miles. He must have come
two.

It was mid-afternoon. The mountains were stark under
a cloudless blue sky. Bank holiday. There were coloured
tents pitched in a field. The hedges grew high on either
side of the lane. All Jimmy could see were the mountains
now and then rearing empty ahead. Four miles was
a long way. His feet were hot and sore. Lucky about that
lift, though. It meant he had enough money to catch a
bus home if he didn't find them. But if they were here
there was only one way to go: straight ahead, follow the
car to the end of the road.

The lane ended suddenly. Branched left and right.
Left was a farm. Right was another lane. Ahead a five-
barred gate and the way to the mountains. Alan's car was
parked in front of it. Jimmy leant against the bonnet.
The metal was burning hot. He'd have to wait until they
came back. If he went to look for them they might come
back whilst he was gone and he'd be left on the flipping
mountains. He climbed the gate and settled in the grass
under a tree. He was hot, then hungry, then thirsty. He
could hear a stream nearby.

Jimmy felt better after a drink but the waiting made

him restless. Sun beating down and brooding mountains hanging all around. He found an apple in a bag under the dashboard and ate it. He could go and look for them. It would be better than just waiting. He took the paper bag down to the stream and mixed mud in it. He wrote: 'WAIT FOR ME, JIMMY' in mud on the side of the car. It dried brown and readable. Jimmy headed for the mountains.

The peat bog at the top of the track squelched under his feet. He had seen the dog first, a white scampering dot on the grey green slope. Then he had seen Jane and Alan right at the top, sprawled on the grass. Jimmy started climbing. He went quietly, avoiding the loose scree. A shadow of a bird drifted over him. He looked up. A buzzard. Jane and Alan were holding hands in the sun. Jane's honey-brown hair was spread out around her. They looked asleep. Jimmy stood over them.

The dog came yapping. Jimmy prodded Alan with his toe.

'Nick wants you.'

Alan rolled over and sat up.

'Nick wants you,' Jimmy said again.

'How did you get here?' Alan looked annoyed.

'I hitched. I met your Mum. She told me you were taking me to the mountains. I thought I'd better come.'

'Good of you. Considerate. Get lost.'

'You've got to get back. And take *her* back.'

'She's asleep,' Alan said.

'I'm not,' Jane murmured her face still buried in the grass. 'I'm not asleep. Is that you, Jimmy?'

'It's him,' Alan said sourly.

'Nick wants you.'

'What the hell for?'

'He wants to talk to you.'

'Why couldn't he have come himself if it's that important?'

'He's in London,' Jimmy said. 'He rang. I thought I ought to come.'

'Jane,' Alan said. 'I'm sorry but we've got to go. There's some kind of panic on.' Jane sat up; clutched her knees, her grey eyes staring at the empty mountains.

'It's nice here. Can't we stay a bit longer?'

'No,' Jimmy said sharply. 'We can't. Come on.'

'It's not that urgent, surely?' Alan said. 'No one's died, have they?'

'No,' Jimmy said. 'But someone might. You or me going home in that car. You or me, Alan boy. Blown to bits like the plane in the sky. Come on, will you.'

Alan pulled Jane to her feet.

'I'm hot,' Jane said.

Her arms were bright red. She looked longingly at the lake, deep and round in the hollow. It reflected the stark slope of the mountain and the blue sky. Alan collected up the remains of their picnic. Jimmy was hot, too. His shirt was sticking to him and his socks felt wet.

'Can't we go to the lake?' Jane asked. It was almost two miles back to the car. The sun was pounding down.

'All right,' Jimmy said. 'But you're not staying there all day. Ten minutes for a paddle and that's all.'

She stared round at the grey green hills quiet under the quiet sky.

'It's nice here.'

'So you said before. Let's go and have this paddle and get home.' Jane ran down to the water. Alan and Jimmy came slowly behind. Alan wanted to wring Jimmy's neck. Murder on the mountain. Bury his body in the lake. If Jimmy was dragging him home for no reason at all, he was going to get a punch up the bracket.

'Push it!' Alan said.
'I *am* pushing.'
'You're not pushing hard enough. She'll never start at that speed.'
'You've switched on, have you?'
'Ha! ha!'
Sweat trickled down Jane's face and the heat of the metal burnt her skin.
'I can't push any more,' Jane said.
'Nor can I,' Jimmy muttered. 'It's all right for him sitting behind the wheel.'
'Push!' Alan said.
'I can't,' Jane said again.
'Give it a rest,' Jimmy said. 'Alan, we're not pushing it up that hill. It's a human impossibility.'
'It can't be the battery. It's a new one.'
'Release the bonnet. I'll have another look.'
Jane stood in the middle of the lane, her hands wide, drawing the coolness of the wind which came from the mountains. Waiting for their shadow to come nearer. Winston watched, bright-eyed from the beige grasses.
'Try the plugs,' Alan said.
'I tried them last time. They're all right. She's firing perfectly. There might be a blockage from the petrol tank.'
The shadow of the mountain was half-way down the track, deep blue purple. The sun was low above the ridge.
'Half past flipping six,' Jimmy muttered. 'I'll try blowing it out.' His hands were black with oil and his face was streaked with dirt. He disconnected the pipe-line. The chink of spanners sounded loud. Cows were lowing not far away. A tractor was droning. Cutting hay. The smell

of it came sweet. Jane sat with her arm round Winston and sniffed contentedly. There were oil marks on Alan's white shirt. Jimmy sucked at the pipe-line and spat on the ground. He stared at it for a moment.

'You great steaming nit!' Jimmy said. 'There's no bloody petrol. No wonder it won't go.'

Alan reached over and switched on the ignition. The petrol gauge registered empty. Alan started laughing.

'I knew she was low. I meant to fill up on the way.'

'It's not funny,' Jimmy said viciously. 'We've been an hour and a half trying to get this damn car to go.'

'I'm sorry.'

'I've been heaving my guts out pushing and there's no flaming petrol.'

'I said I'm sorry. I'll see if they've got any at the farm.'

'You see,' Jimmy said. 'And hurry up. I've had nothing to eat since breakfast except one rotten apple.'

'Whose fault is that?' Alan asked as he started back along the lane.

It was five past eight by the time Alan had walked to Brecon and back to fetch a gallon of petrol. Jimmy wandered round and round the car, restlessly glancing at his watch, restlessly glancing at the sky. Jane and Winston sat quite still among the feathered grass beside the road watching the shadow line creep down the mountains, seeing the sun gradually sink lower until it was hovering above the ridge. Alan tipped the petrol. The smell drifted towards her. Strong. Jane smiled.

'Get in,' Jimmy told her.

'I'll put the hood on,' Alan said as he screwed on the cap.

'It's not cold,' Jimmy said.

'It might be before we get home.'

Jane touched her burning arms.

'The wind is chilly.'

She scooped up the dog and waited for Alan to fix the hood. Jimmy looked at his watch. Quarter past eight. Hurry up, man. For Pete's sake hurry up. Twenty past eight. The car went slowly along the narrow lane. They met a Land-Rover coming up and had to back into a gateway and let it pass. Half past eight. Twenty to nine when they reached the main road. Jimmy relaxed a little. Get up a bit of speed now and they'd be back before dark. He stretched out his legs in the space behind the seats. Through the window the mountains had cut the sunset in half but the sky was still pale blue.

'I'm sorry Jane,' Alan said. 'You're going to be late home. I hope you won't get into trouble.'

Jane smiled. 'It doesn't matter.'

In Brecon Alan filled up with petrol then crawled through the town, held up by the traffic lights and the amount of traffic. Speed rattled the canvas hood as the car rushed down the hill. Seventy along the flat. Jimmy watched the speedometer with satisfaction. They caught up with a fifty-ton transporter doing twenty-five. The flow of traffic the other way was continual. The road was narrow and winding. They followed it all the way to Abergavenny. The sinking sun gleamed on the mirror. Alan fumed. What a lousy end to the day. Everything turned sour.

In Abergavenny, too, the traffic lights were against them. The Sugar Loaf towered above them and the sun had completely gone. But it was only the mountains that hid it. It was still there, just below the ridge. Nine-fifty. Almost an hour and a half to come twenty-nine miles. The road wound down, then up, wooded on either side. A dark gloomy tunnel cut through trees. Gnats danced, caught the last light on flickering wings.

'God, I'm hungry,' Jimmy muttered.

'We can stop,' Alan said. 'And get something to eat. We'll get it in the neck anyway. Another half-hour won't matter.'

'Don't bother. I'll wait till we get home.'

Just get home, man.

The white sports car ate up the swift miles. The sky was a deeper blue. Growing dark in the east. Still pale in the west. The signpost said the motorway was one mile. Jimmy heaved a sigh of relief. They'd make it yet. The car swerved wildly and stopped.

'Guess what?' Alan said.

'What?' Jimmy said angrily.

'A puncture.'

Jimmy clenched his fist. A flat tyre was all he needed.

'I suppose you've got a spare?'

'In the boot,' Alan said.

'Well, don't just sit there. Let's change the blasted thing.'

'Sorry Jane,' Alan said. 'Can you get out and let Jimmy through? I might want some help.'

The car was low on the grass. They hunted for a length of wood to lever it up. Jimmy used a fence pole. It was rotten and snapped. They searched among the trees. Jimmy strained down on a broken branch and Alan slipped the jack underneath. Then the wheel bolts were rusty. It took brute force before they came undone. Brute force and twenty minutes. Alan put the wheel in the boot and carried the spare round to Jimmy. It was flat.

'Hell's bells and buckets of blood,' Jimmy muttered. 'This is the last time I come out for a ride with you.

'I didn't ask you to come,' Alan reminded him.

Jimmy started pumping. The hiss and sigh of air came slow, regular, faster. Jimmy pumped furiously. Cars flashed by them with stabbing headlamps.

'Poor Jane,' Alan said. 'I've landed her right in the soup. She was supposed to back by nine.'

Jimmy looked up at the sky and realised it was dark. His aching leg stopped and his stomach felt hollow and tight with tension. It was dark and the stars were shining.

'I'll take over,' Alan said.

Jimmy leant against the car waiting for the sick feeling in his stomach to ease off. The hiss hiss of air being forced into the tyre went on. A different rhythm. Cars went by with rushes of speed.

'Where is she?' Jimmy asked heavily.

'Jane? I don't suppose she's far away.'

Alan pumped and pumped.

'Where is she?'

'Around somewhere.'

Alan kicked the tyre.

'That ought to hold till we get home.'

'*If* we get home,' Jimmy muttered.

'Surely nothing else *can* go wrong?' Alan tightened the screws on the wheel.

'Do you know why Nick rang?' Jimmy asked.

'I thought you said he wanted me.'

'Aye. That's what I said. I told him you'd gone out with Jane and he nearly hit the roof.'

Alan straightened up. 'How petty can you get? You came all that way to tell me Nick didn't approve of me taking Jane out? Why didn't you keep your mouth shut in the first place? You knew damn well Nick put his foot down.'

'And a pity you didn't put your foot down. We'd have been home by now.'

'You could have stayed at home, Jimmy boy. It's not my fault you're here. It's not my fault you've had nothing to eat. You and Nick want your heads banging together. Put the jack in the boot. We'll be home in less than an hour.'

'Man, I couldn't give a hoot who you take out, but not her. Unless you want to be blown sky high?'

'You off on that track again?' There was just the sound of cars going by. Jimmy couldn't see Jane.

'Nick rang to say I was probably right,' Jimmy said.

'What?'

'I'm right. About the washing machine and the telly. That plane. She blew it up. It was her. Stars, that's how she does it. She drinks up the power of stars like a vampire drinks blood.'

'And Nick believes you?'

'That's why he rang.'

'Then he's a great big demented Scottish twit.'

'I gave him that slide I pinched from Fanny Cotterel's.'

'I don't care what you gave him. If he believes that, he's as nutty as you are.' Alan slammed the boot.

'If you'd just listen . . .'

'I don't want to listen. You're making Jane into a monster. Something inhuman. It can't be done, Jimmy boy. And I'm not going to listen.'

'So where is she then?' Jimmy demanded. 'Where is she? Around somewhere? You bet she is. She's around. She's gazing at the stars. That's what she's doing. She's filling her tiny mind with star power and when she gets back she'll be loaded with it. She's got things inside her. She got them from the rabbit. They blast out star power, boy. We've got to take her home in the car, I'd rather walk.'

'Then walk!' Alan snapped.

Walk? Twelve miles? At this time of night? Jimmy climbed behind the seat and waited.

'Jane!' Alan shouted. 'We're ready.' There was no

answer. Only the sound of wheels on the road, only the warm smell of traffic fumes.

'When you find her,' Jimmy shouted. 'Tell her I don't want to die.'

Alan walked down the road. The sky was still light over the mountains. They were dark silhouettes someone had painted. Overhead were the stars, brilliant yellow. All that power pouring down. Jane was standing by a field gate looking up at the sky. A thousand, thousand stars shining on her eyes. There had been a flash of light when the rabbit screamed. Heat to burn its leg, melt the metal trap and set it free. It had bitten Jane. What things had Jane got inside her?

'Jane,' Alan said. 'We're going now.'

She still stared at the sky.

'They're beautiful,' Jane said. 'Don't you think so? The stars are the most beautiful things in the world.'

'Out of the world,' Alan said and caught her hand. 'Come on, girl. Home we go. I'm sorry your day was spoilt.'

'But it was lovely,' Jane said. She looked up again. 'Lovely.'

A car flashed by. Speed and fumes and engine noise. Alan felt the hand he was holding stiffen.

'I hate it,' Jane said.

Behind came the rattle of dog's claws on the road. Winston whined.

Alan's hands gripping the wheel were slick with sweat. He couldn't forget what Jimmy had said. It kept going round and round in his mind, endless circles like the orbits of stars. Her hand had stiffened when the car went by. She had been staring at the stars, filling her mind with power. The stars are the most beautiful things in the world. The most powerful. Things in her head, Jimmy said. Loaded with power. Tell her I don't want to die.

The car lights coming towards him hurt his eyes. Flashes of brilliant light, returning to darkness. His every nerve was stretched taut. The road was straight and wide all the way to Monmouth. Fast. Home was twenty minutes away.

They went through the lighted town. Under orange glowing street lamps. Alan glanced at Jane. Her face was colourless. Drawn. Her eyes were staring straight ahead. She was clutching the dog so tightly her knuckles shone. He sensed she was tensed to breaking point. Every time he changed gear, revved the engine, her tension grew. Why? She'd been all right all day. What had the stars done to her?

He slowed to turn on to the bridge. The engine faltered. Alan pressed his foot on the accelerator. The car crawled across, the noise was harsh and echoing. She wasn't picking up speed. He started to climb the wooded hills that began Langdon Forest. Again the engine faltered. Again the roar when he pressed his foot down. The speed dropped. The engine sound increased. The head-lamps stabbed the dark tunnel of road. A sign shone red. Bends for two miles. Alan was sweating. What was wrong with the bloody car now? Choke, splutter, roar. Vibrations shaking his body. Loud slow revs, no speed. The accelerator was right down to the floor. Winston howled and fell by his feet.

'Stop it!' Jane screamed. She had covered her ears with her hands. Alan willed the car to go, slower, slower, up and up. Noise and noise, and noise and noise. He could hear nothing else. He could think of nothing else. The noise drove all thought away. Just to the top. A few yards more then down into Langdon.

'Stop it!' Jane screamed. 'Stop it! Stop it! Stop it!'

Jimmy caught her round the neck.

'No! No you don't!'

The car gained the top. There was a flash. The tension snapped. Heat came in a blast, stifling, burning, enveloping them. Alan let go of the wheel and covered his face. The car keeled across the road. There was a bang. The plastic window splintered and disintegrated. Alan struck his head against the framework of the hood. He felt it give way. He was flung into nothing, out of the heat and flames into nothing. Blackness and nothing. Stars shining in the black sky above him. Nothing.

14

'THERE's no way of knowing where they come from. There's a billion billion stars out there; how could we possibly know? Some planet in another arm of our galaxy? One unshielded from infra-red radiation or ultra-violet radiation? We could guess but never know.'

Alan closed his eyes. He'd heard it all before from Jimmy and he hadn't believed it. Now it was Nick's turn and he still wouldn't believe it, but his head ached too much to argue. He let Nick talk on.

'Their molecular structure is complex. At one time they must have had bodies, maybe like ours. But they built machines, came to depend on them and eventually couldn't live without them. We think they became integrated with machines.'

'What's that mean?' Jimmy asked. Words of more than two syllables were beyond Jimmy's vocabulary.

'Part and parcel,' Nick said. 'It would have taken a few million years, a slow process of evolution, but they lost their limbs and senses and ended up as just a brain inside a machine. They couldn't live without machines. They were totally and utterly dependent on them. They were just a core of intelligence within metal.'

Alan sank deeper in the pillows. Once upon a time and they all lived happily ever after. Which master mind had made up this little story? Jimmy? And if Nick believed it he ought to have B.F. after his name, not M.D.

'Taking energy direct from whatever sun they lived under is a unique form of metabolism,' Nick went on, 'but they do it. Direct energy, as much as they need, no waste products, no digestion. They can also reverse their metabolic process, exude energy, enough heat and power to melt metal. We assume that's how they escaped from their metal bodies.'

We? Alan opened one eye. He saw Miss Cotterel standing at the end of the bed. What was she doing here? Inspiration if Nick dried up?

'They were merely cells, then,' Nick said. 'Neurons. Each one part of its original brain but separated. They were small enough to float in air, small enough to escape from the gravitational pull of their planet and drift into space. They would be dormant in a vacuum but their knowledge and intelligence would be there when favourable conditions returned them to consciousness: the thin air of some upper atmosphere or the comparative warmth of a nearby star.'

Alan hadn't realised Nick had such a fascinating mind. Ingenious invention. Still, the idea was pinched. The idea was Jimmy's, elaborated on. He could hear the rattle of cups on a tea trolley down the corridor.

'It may have been only chance that brought them to Earth. It may have been design, a systematic search of the galaxy for a world which supported life. They could have floated through space for a thousand years or a million years. They were dormant and time wouldn't matter. But they came here, and here was everything they had lost. Minds within bodies, bodies which would obey minds. Here was seeing, and hearing, tasting, smelling and touching. The five senses they had lost aeons of years ago. They wanted to live again, not merely exist. They wanted to be within a body, to share the sensations of material being.'

And the wolf said : 'I'll huff and I'll puff and I'll blow your house down.' What's he stopped for?

'Are you asleep?' Nick asked.

'I will be in a minute,' Alan muttered. Nick leaned over him. Alan didn't see him, he sensed him, his shadow darkening the sunlight which came through the window.

'Well, go on,' Alan said. 'This is leading up to something. Don't stop now. I want to know the end before I drop off.'

'These cells are very small,' Nick said slowly. 'But they can't pass through solid matter.'

So they float, Alan thought, without senses. They float among the petals of flowers which have no scent and no sweetness, among the invisible leaves of a tree, like sheen on the feathers of a bird they can't hear singing, like sunlight in a jam jar broken to a shifting mist of rainbow colours. Floating like he was; unreal if it weren't for the pain in his head.

'They were there that night when the rabbit was caught in the trap,' Nick said.

Alan realised the significance. The story was changing from fictitious events to real happenings.

'A trapped animal wasn't much use to them. They utilised their energy to create heat, to melt the metal trap and set it free. They entered the rabbit's body through the wound on its leg, diffused through its blood system to its brain. They must have realised before long that the beast would die. Perhaps they didn't realise soon enough, not before the wound had congealed and shut them in. But they had enough control over the animal's reflexes to make it act against its nature, bite its own lip and let them go, bite a dog and let them gain another body, bite Jane and let them pass into her.'

'No!' Alan choked.

'He hasn't finished yet,' Jimmy said. 'He hasn't told you how Jane blows up machines. Go on, Nick. Tell him about Jane.'

Jane had those things inside her? Is that what Nick

was saying? Is that what Nick believed? Expected *him* to believe?

'Jane,' Nick said, 'wasn't an animal but a creature with intelligence of her own. There was nothing Jane couldn't experience, nothing she couldn't do, nothing she couldn't know. They made her live every moment to the full so that whatever she felt they would share her feelings. They could hear music Jane had not even bothered to listen to. Now she had to listen because they wanted her to. They appreciated music. Who wouldn't after being deaf for God knows how long? They taught Jane to appreciate it, too. They could even make her play a musical instrument she had never touched before. They made her play your piano. And dance. Jimmy told me about that dance. That was how Jane could suddenly dance. Not her, Alan, but them. For Jane everything became more vivid; her feelings and senses were intensified because for them it was all new and they were part of Jane. They were being re-born through Jane.

'But they still needed starlight. Starlight provided them with energy. Without starlight their animation was suspended, their intelligence dormant and their experiences non-existent. They could draw in the power of starlight through Jane's eyes. They were part of her. They shared her feelings, she shared their instinct. She had to see the stars. If you look at it from their point of view it was a marvellous arrangement; ideal symbiosis. They must have been very happy for a while.'

Like a marriage ceremony. Congratulations! I hope you are very happy. They were inside Jane. Sharing her feelings. Jane's feelings. For him? It was revolting! The thought was revolting. Happy? Hell, oh hell!

'The only trouble was that this is a mechanised world,' Nick was saying. 'We've already made machines and begun to depend on them. We don't walk where we can take the car. They knew all about machines and what they could do. They'd seen it happen before. The day would come when we wouldn't be able to live without machines. We'd forget how to use our limbs, our eyes, our senses. Easier to let machines do things. We'd become integrated with machines. End up as just minds inside them. Jane would. Jane would lose the power of her body until all she had left was a tiny core of intelligence. She and they would be sealed inside a metal case. They'd be nothingness and they'd only just escaped from being nothingness. They saw history repeating itself and they retaliated. They reversed their energy process, poured out the starlight they had taken in, destroyed machines. They expended energy in flashes of heat and power until it was gone and Jane craved to see the stars again, replace it for them and re-animate them.'

'Who thought that one up?' Alan fought against believing.

'It could be called a hypothetical deduction. We took everything we knew and pieced it together. They might even have been human. Once.'

Once! They weren't now though. They weren't even Earthly, let alone human. And she had them inside her. Jane did. Sharing her feelings. Sharing everything she did. Hearing everything. What he'd said to her that day on the mountains. The thought filled him with sick horror.

'No!' The skin on his forehead was pulled tight, held together by a line of stitches. It was some sort of joke. Something they'd made up. To see how gullible he was, how much he'd believe. Not that. He couldn't believe that.

'No! No! No!'

'You could say Dr Mackenzie and I pooled our information,' Miss Cotterel said. Her voice came from miles away. She was a tweed-clad statue which never moved. They'd conjured her up to try and make him believe.

'No!'

Nick touched his hand.

'Easy. You've had a bang on the head.' The booming voice came to back him up.

'Sorry about your accident, boy. If you'd stayed away as you were told it wouldn't have happened. You young people never listen. Lucky you weren't killed. Not altogether Jane's fault. She couldn't control them. I knew that.'

The room was spinning round.

'You knew!' Jimmy said accusingly to Miss Cotterel.

Jimmy was hazy on a chair by the bed. His arm was in white plaster right up to his shoulder.

'Oh, yes. I knew. Found the rabbit. Wanted to know what made it bite. Dissected it. Found the cells inside. Noticed they didn't like machines. Put them on the refrigerator.'

'Vic did, too,' Nick said. Alan wondered vaguely who Vic was.

'Noticed it in Winston first,' Miss Cotterel said. 'Suddenly took a dislike to the car. Scared stiff of it. The traffic in the street. Scared stiff. Never was before. Took me several days to realise why. Thought of the girl then. That rabbit had bitten her too. It worried me.'

'You knew,' Jimmy said. 'Why in hell's name didn't you do something?'

'Did all I could, James. Precious little but keep an eye on her. Nothing I could do until her grandmother met with the accident. She came to me, knew I knew. I was glad to give her a home. Been on my own except for Randolph and Winston since Leonard died. Thought it would be interesting from the scientific point of view. Might even be able to communicate with them through the girl. Kept some of them. Tried to get through to them but there was no way. It was different with Jane.'

'Is that all she was?' Jimmy asked. 'A flipping scientific experiment?'

'Didn't know I'd get fond of her. And it was dangerous. She couldn't control them. They were too powerful. Had the shutters fixed on the windows. Kept her away from the stars. Kept the cells dormant. All I could do, keep them dormant. She was all right until someone let her out.'

'So now it's our fault?'.

'And what else could I do? If you know, James, then I'm prepared to listen.'

'You could try getting rid of them,' Jimmy said.

'How?'

'I don't know. How would I know?'

'You don't eh? That makes two of us. Any other suggestion?'

'It's not true,' Alan whispered. It was something he had dreamt, not something that had happened. A science fiction story someone had made up. Someone had told him and he thought it was real.

'Take it easy, Alan,' Nick said. 'Lie back. You've only just come round.'

'It's not true.'

'I'm sorry, but it is.'

'You don't know. You can't know.'

'We've X-rayed Jane,' Nick said. 'There's a shadow on her brain the size of a ten penny piece. The doctor who examined her wants to send her to Bristol for an immediate operation. He thinks it's a tumour.'

'Jane's here?'

'Downstairs. She had a bang on the head, too. She's still unconscious.'

Alan touched the bandage around his head. 'How long

have I been out?'

'Sixteen hours.'

Outside the window the bright sun of Sunday afternoon filtered through the branches of a tree in spots of
brilliant yellow.

'I feel sick,' Alan said.

Nick gave him a bowl. Alan stared at its white clinical
surface for several minutes then put it on the locker.

'How long will I have to stop here?'

'A couple of days.'

'And Jimmy?'

'He can go.'

'Thanks very much,' Jimmy said. 'I'm due to play
cricket on Wednesday.'

'And Jane?'

'She stays,' Nick said. He looked at Miss Cotterel. 'I'd
like Jane to come to London.'

'You think something can be done, Dr Mackenzie?'

'I would like to try a course of antibiotic treatment. A
new one has just been developed. There's a chance it
could destroy the cells but I will need your permission to
use it.'

'No,' Alan said. 'You can't use that.'

'Be quiet! This is nothing to do with you. Perhaps you
will come into the office, Miss Cotterel, where we can
discuss it.'

'You can't use that on Jane,' Alan hissed. 'It's not
proved. It's only been tested on rats. Jane's not a rat.
She's a human being.'

'I'll speak to you later, old lad.'

'Don't old lad me. You don't care what it does to her,
do you? First she was a scientific experiment, now she's a
flipping medical guinea pig.'

'Get some shut-eye!'

'Do it to the dog.'

'Winston's dead,' Miss Cotterel said. 'He was killed in the accident.'

Alan felt a wave of sickness wash through him.

'Try it on yourself then, but not Jane.'

'You want me to leave those things in her head?' Nick asked. 'I'll talk to you later.' He strode away down the ward.

Jimmy leaned back in the chair and stretched out his legs.

'He doesn't care who he tries it on,' Alan said, 'as long as it's someone. I was driving the car. The clutch went. Revs but no speed. The clutch went. I was driving and I lost control.'

'You still won't listen, will you? You didn't lose control, man. Jane blew the flipping thing up.'

'I was driving.'

'She blew it up.'

'Prove it.'

Jimmy spread his hands. 'She did it. I told you to come home. I told you what Nick said. You should have listened.'

'I came.'

'Aye, you came. Half past eleven at night and all the stars blazing down.'

'It could kill her,' Alan said. 'That biotic. Nick doesn't know what effect it could have.'

'And she could have killed me,' Jimmy said.

Tell her I don't want to die. It was true. It was true. Everything was true. He didn't want to accept it but he had to. It was repulsive. Cells inside her that weren't her own. He had to accept it.

'You'll be here,' Jimmy said. 'The two of you together. You and Jane. You'll be able to comfort her, won't you? Hold her hand and tell her not to worry. You think we're all callous. You think we don't think of Jane at all.

143

How she feels. She'll need all the help you can give her.'

Alan bent forward and rested his head on his knees. Have an alien intelligence watching him through Jane's eyes? Listening to what he said? He didn't even want to go near her. The horror made him heave.

Jimmy thrust the bowl in his hands.

'Nick's not daft,' Jimmy said. 'He knows what he's doing. Someone's got to do something.'

15

NICK slammed down the telephone. He'd been in a bad temper all day. Anna had gone out for the day with the local flower arrangers' society and he'd had to get the dinner. It was yellow haddock and it had boiled dry. Stuck to the bottom of the saucepan. It was still soaking in the sink with the rest of the washing-up. Someone ought to do it. He went back into the garden. Alan was lying on the lawn with a newspaper over his face. Half the grass was neatly mown.

'It wouldn't have hurt you to carry on,' Nick snapped as he set the blades turning.

'I'm convalescing. Mum told you to get a motor one. Who was that?'

'The garage. They wanted a hundred and twenty pounds. I told them to keep the car.'

Alan rustled the newspaper away and sat up. His head thumped and the sunlight hurt his eyes. 'You what?'

'I told them to keep the damned car.' The back of Nick's shirt was wet with sweat.

'You can't do that. It's my car.'

'It was.'

'You can't just let the garage have it.'

'I'm not paying a hundred and twenty pounds to have it mended. You must think I'm made of money.'

'You knew it would cost a bit. You said you'd pay.'

'A bit! A hundred and twenty pounds is more than a bit. I haven't got that amount of money to hand out. It's only a hundred less than the car cost.'

'You rotten stingy Scotsman.'

'I paid eighty for your mother's washing machine a couple of months ago. If it had been fifty it would have been different. You can manage without a car.'

'Mum bought me that car.'

'I know. She'd have been more sensible to keep her money.'

'It was a bribe. To persuade me to let her marry you. She wouldn't have married you if I hadn't agreed.'

'Is that so?'

'Yes.'

'Well you're stuck with me now and she won't be buying you another.' Nick pushed the mower a few yards. Grass flew over Alan's legs.

'So you're not paying then?'

'No I'm not.'

'Right! I'll ask Mum then.'

Nick stopped pushing.

'What did you say?'

'I said I'll ask Mum. She'll pay.'

'Oh no she won't because you won't be asking her.'

'I will.'

'You won't.'

'She's my mother. If I want to ask her then I shall.'

'Anna will not be giving you a hundred and twenty pounds, because I won't let her.'

'You can't stop her.'

'She's my wife,' Nick said. 'She'll do as she's told. You've had it easy up to now, boy. Everything you've wanted you've been given. You haven't had to work for anything. It's been handed you on a plate. Your mother bought you that car, taxed it, insured it and I suspect pays for the petrol even though she denies it. She's waited on you hand foot and finger all your life. Your mother's been damned good to you to the point of stupidity and what have you ever done for her, eh?'

Alan clenched his fist.

'I let her marry you.'

'Noble of you. You've done nothing for your mother. Nothing! You never do anything in the house. There's a sink full of washing-up in there now. You never do anything in the garden. Look at the weeds. You have your friends in all hours of the night and expect her to cook for them. I've never heard you thank her. It's time you pulled your socks up, son.'

'Don't son me. You're not my father.'

'Thank God!'

'Yes. You can say that again.'

'There's seven weeks holiday coming up soon. Have you got yourself a job?'

'Not yet.'

'No. Not yet. You prefer to loaf around on your backside composing music or listening to those rubbishy pop records. That factory in Hasley pays twenty pounds a week to students. If you want another car, Alan, then you damn well earn it. And if you think I'm keeping you in idleness for the next five years whilst you drift through university then think again. Just think again.'

Alan stood up, brushed the sour damp grass from his legs.

'Mum and me were all right until you came along.'

The mower made a gentle whirring noise.

'And now I am here things are changing. You can't wind your mother round your little finger any more because I can stop you. You don't like it, do you? You're not the only plum in the pie any more. And whilst we're doing the ironing, what about Jane?'

'Leave her out of it.'

Nick came nearer. His eyes were as hard as steel.

'I asked you about Jane and I want an answer.'

'I know what you think,' Alan said, breathing hard.

147

'You think she's not good enough. She's not good enough to go out with the great Dr Mackenzie's stepson.'

'My God!' Nick said. 'Is that what you think?'

'It's true, isn't it?'

'Your conceit is incredible.'

'You said I was to leave her alone, Nick. You said it.'

'Jane is good enough to go out with any man's son.'

'Except with me? I got warned off. I got told to leave her alone.'

'And that was for one reason only. To avoid Miss Cotterel taking you to court. Jane's a nice girl. But she's sick. Miss Cotterel knew that. She knew what starlight could do to Jane. She had to keep her inside. And if it meant taking you to court she was prepared to do that. You let her out once. The woman did not intend it to happen again. But since you took no notice of either me or Miss Cotterel I'll ask you again : what about Jane?'

'Nothing,' Alan muttered. 'Leave her alone.'

Jane wasn't Jane any more. She was something else. Something alien and unacceptable. He could never look at her again and feel the same. Whenever he looked at her he would see something else : brain cells.

'Nothing,' Nick murmured. 'So now we know. And now you're going to know. Jane's been lying in hospital for two weeks. I have seen her every day and every day she asked me where you were, how you were, if you were coming to see her, when you were coming. She'll know now what you think of her. Nothing!'

'I'm not the only one,' Alan said. 'There's Jimmy.'

'Jimmy's been to see her most days after school.'

'That's not what I meant.'

'I don't care what you meant. As far as I'm concerned, boy, you've fallen from your white horse. You dared to condemn Jimmy for his past treatment of Jane. You dared to condemn Miss Cotterel who gave her a home and did everything humanly possible to protect her. You even condemn me for wanting to treat her and yet you can't even go and see her, talk to her, try and help her. It's time you took a long, hard look at your own behaviour, Alan.'

Alan stared stonily at the neat blue border of lobelia around the lawn. The edges needed trimming. There were weeds hiding the lettuces and a sink full of washing-up to be done. The scar on his forehead was tight and hurting and what Nick said brought gall to the back of his throat. Go and see Jane? Talk to her? Try and help? Nick didn't know what he was asking.

'I'm not taking any more,' Alan said.

'Then get out of my sight,' Nick said.

The heat was too stifling to move. The air was languid and heavy. Why didn't he have a heart attack and drop dead? The sound of the mower went on and on. Even in the kitchen Alan could hear it over the sound of water running. He scrubbed at the brown mess in the bottom of the pan. The phone rang.

Alan stood in the doorway with soapsuds dripping from his mother's apron.

'Phone!' Alan shouted.

'Well, answer it. Or do you want me to fetch the wheelchair and push you?'

Alan hated Nick.

'It's for you. And for Pete's sake don't keep on. I'll land you one in a minute.'

Nick banged down the handle of the mower.

'Don't go away! I heard that!'

Nick was on the phone a long time. Alan left the plates to drain and went on with mowing the lawn. He listened to the sound. Concentrated on the sight of the blades turning round and round, spraying out grass. He didn't want to think. Nick came out with his jacket on.

'Tell Anna I've gone out. I don't know when I'll be back.'

'I've done the washing-up.'

'Really?'

'What's wrong?'

Nick hesitated. 'It's Jane.'

'Jane?'

'I told her this morning she was coming to London with me on Monday for a course of antibiotics. She's disappeared.'

'Disappeared?'

'Left the hospital. Some time this afternoon. No one saw her.'

'You told her about those things inside her head? I thought you decided not to, you and Miss Cotterel. I thought you were going to spare her the horror of knowing. She's probably drowning herself in the river.'

'I didn't tell her.'

'Maybe Jimmy did.'

'Well,' Nick said. 'We know for sure it wasn't you. All of a sudden Jane has become too repulsive for you to even look at.'

'No!'

Nick regarded him.

'No!' Alan said. 'It's not that. It's not!'

'Isn't it? You could have helped her, Alan. You above all could have helped her.'

'I'm sorry.'

Nick shrugged and went to the car. Alan heard the engine start. Saw the blue saloon back through the gates of Amberley House. He ran after it. Nick wound down the window.

'Nick, where are you going?'

'To look for her.'

Alan braced himself. 'I'll come too.'

150

16

ALAN opened the kitchen door very quietly so as not to wake his mother. He groped for the light switch.

'God, I'm tired,' Nick said. 'Come on, Alan. Get inside. Let's make a cup of tea.'

'There's no light,' Alan said. 'Bulb must have gone. I'll find another and you put the kettle on.' He went into the hall. There was no light there, either.

'Bloody hell! A flipping fuse gone. Nick, there must be a fuse gone.'

'I can hear you. Talk quieter or you'll wake Anna. I'll have a look. Feel round in the pantry and find the primus stove. We can boil a kettle on that whilst we're waiting. Where's the torch?'

'In the sideboard drawer.'

Every small noise seemed twice as loud in the quiet house. Nick knocked into something and swore. Alan rattled among the empty jam jars on the pantry floor and dragged out the camping stove. A small blue flame made a circle of light on the kitchen ceiling. It would take the kettle a long time to boil. Alan cut some bread, found the cheese and pickled onions. It wasn't as dark as he had thought. The night outside gave a certain amount of light. Starlight, Alan thought, and shivered.

'There's nothing wrong with the fuse that I can see,' Nick said.

'Must be a cut then,' Alan said. 'They usually let us know. I've put out some cheese and pickles. The tea won't be long.'

His hands smelled of the woods, earth, and bark, and

ivy leaves, hunting through the woods all night for Jane.

'Ugh!' Nick said. 'You put marge on this bread.'

'Well, it was dark, wasn't it? I couldn't tell the difference.'

The kettle boiled over with a hiss. Alan made the tea. Scrunched onions whilst it brewed and then poured out.

'You're working well tonight,' Nick said. 'I must be getting old.'

Working well. Hunting through the woods. Calling her name. Hoping she wouldn't come so that he wouldn't see her, wouldn't have to speak to her, wouldn't be reminded of who she was. Walking all night under the trees and under the stars, dodging branches, listening to the searchers all around him. Calling her so that he wouldn't have to think about her. Calling till his throat was sore. Jane!

'There's a car stopped outside,' Nick said. 'Go and see who it is before they bang on the door.'

Alan went out into the night, into the dark before the dawn. Three-thirty by his watch. He saw the car beyond the gate, a flashing blue light.

'Dr Mackenzie?' someone said.

Inside the car a wireless was talking.

'He's in the house. We've just got back. Have you found her?'

'No. We were wondering if you had. The station asked us to check. We're patrolling the roads. Not much hope of finding her tonight, though.'

'There's some tea made if you want some.'

'Thanks, son.'

Alan returned to the house and left the door open. He heard boots coming up the path.

'Found her?' Nick asked.

The two policemen seemed to fill the kitchen.

'Nowp. No sign of her. We'll get reinforcements in the

morning. Be easier to search in daylight. For a sick girl she's disappeared remarkably quickly.'

'Her illness hasn't affected her physical strength,' Nick said. 'But it's imperative she has treatment immediately.'

'Aye. We were told. It's been one of those nights.' The policeman glanced at the ceiling where the light usually was. 'There's a panic on the other side of the river too. An explosion in the nuclear power station. Five counties without electricity. Don't know what happened exactly. We heard it over the radio. Just blew up apparently. Well, thanks very much for the tea. I should get some sleep if I were you, Doctor. We'll find that little lady for you. We'd best call at the bungalow now, George. See if she's turned up there. Trouble with Langdon Forest is that it's big. Trees and quarries everywhere. But we'll find her.'

Alan closed the door behind them. Heard the gate slam. Heard the car pull away and the silence come back.

'She's really done it this time,' Nick said. 'A nuclear power station. That's what you call going out with a bang. All I hope is they find her quickly. She can't go on.'

'No,' Alan said. 'No, she can't go on.' He pulled on his sweater and went to the door.

'Where are you going?' Nick asked.

Alan paused with his hand on the handle.

'I'm going to find Jane.'

'Leave it. You've been out all night. Leave it to them. They'll find her.'

'I know where she is.'

Nick ran his fingers through his hair. He looked tired and haggard.

'You're sure?'

Somewhere high. You can see the river and the power

station on the other side. At night it's like a fairy castle reflecting on the water. It makes you feel powerful until you look down and the drop makes you feel sick.

'I think I'm sure,' Alan said. 'I think she's at Langdon Point. It's worth a try.'

Nick hauled himself to his feet.

'I'll come with you.'

'Finish your tea,' Alan said. 'I'll go on my own.'

Jimmy was restless and couldn't sleep. The birds started singing before it was light. He dressed and went to the window. Damn things want shooting and old mother Morgan's cock along with them. I'll wring its neck one of these days. Make a good Sunday dinner that would. Tough though. A couple of pale plump pigeons would be better. Jimmy groped downstairs and took his gun from behind the pantry door. It would be light soon, light enough to see pigeons. He took half a dozen cartridges from the drawer and let himself out. A police car was just pulling away from Amberley House. Hello? What's going on?

He went between the trees. There was a gleam of dawn ahead and something moved in the corner of his eye. He skewed round. Someone moving somewhere. Jimmy ducked low. Who was it? He skimmed the sky-line. There! It looked like Alan. Where was he off to this time in the morning? Jimmy waited until he'd gone then followed a short distance behind. Where was Alan going? What had a police car been doing at Amberley House? He saw the car again, going down Green Bottom with flashing lights. Just left the Battery House. Something was definitely going on.

Alan went up the twisting path to the railway line. Across the line and up into the woods. Jimmy followed, soft-footed in his plimsolls. Should have put wellingtons on. His socks were soaked with dew. There was a translucent gleam about everything and the sky was pearly pink in front, dark behind. Shepherd's warning. Didn't follow though. Jimmy knew it was going to be a fine day. He sank deep into the moss of Langdon Woods. Only one place Alan could be going. The Point. What for? To watch the blooming sunrise? Jimmy crept on, silent as a shadow through the bracken fronds. Pigeons didn't matter now.

Alan looked down at her curled up on the grass in the corner of a roofless room. The sun gleamed in a single slanting ray through the empty shell of window and dropped gold on her hair. Grass grew around her, dewed fronds that trembled as she breathed. The pale blue nightdress clung to her. In the yellow oak trees dawn birds poured music from their throats. Alan watched her. The movement of breathing, rise and fall, which disturbed the grass and a tendril of her hair. She wasn't alien. She wasn't some monster. She was Jane. He should have known that. He touched her cold damp hair.

'Jane!'

Her grey eyes flew open. He saw fear, an animal's fear. She sat up and cringed against the wall. Alan stepped back. Some horrible alien intelligence was staring at him through her eyes. Hating him. Knowing what he wanted to do, what Nick wanted to do. Driving Jane to destroy and run like a hunted animal to save themselves from being destroyed. It wasn't Jane he saw now, it was them. It wasn't Jane he talked to.

'Listen to me.'

'No! Go away!'

Everything he'd ever said to her, every word had been overheard. Every moment they'd spent together had been watched. They'd seen and heard it all from inside

155

Jane's head. That day on the mountains. They'd known how she felt . . . there hadn't been just him and Jane, there had been them as well. What else was it but repulsive? Alan turned his eyes away from her, through the window to the dew-drying world, the yellow summer trees, the grey drift of river and the misted hills on the other side.

'You've got to listen. You've got to come back home. You've got to go to London with Nick.'

'No!' Even in her voice he heard them.

'You must.'

'No!'

It was a sob of defiance. It was them defending their right to live.

'Nick will look after you. He'll see you're all right.'

'I don't want to.'

'Why not?'

The cuckoo called loud over all the others. Birds singing and screaming all round. Alan wanted to scream, too. You've got to go. You've got to get rid of those things in your head because if you don't I can't look at you or touch you again. I'll be seeing and touching them and I can't. I can't. They're loathsome brain cells.

'Why not?' Alan repeated roughly.

'It's wrong to destroy life,' Jane said.

They knew. They were in her mind and they knew. They knew Nick would destroy them and somehow Jane knew, too. She was protecting them. Things from outer space, parasites. She wanted them to stay.

'There's nothing you can do,' Alan said. 'The police are out looking for you. They'll find you. They'll make you go with Nick.'

'No,' Jane whispered. 'No. Please no. You can't let them. Help me.'

She turned her head to the wall and cried. Help me. Not

her but them. Alan couldn't. He watched her for a moment. He couldn't touch her. He turned to go. Jimmy was standing where the doorway used to be.

'You're leaving her?'

'She won't listen.'

Jimmy didn't say anything.

'I tried. She wouldn't listen.'

'I heard you.'

'How did you know I was here?'

'I followed you. You were leaving her? Crying?'

Alan looked back at Jane crouching against the wall. Everything rotten he was, but he couldn't touch her.

Jimmy pushed past him. That was Jane crying. Not anyone else. Not anything else. Not cells or power. Just Jane. He pulled her away from the wall. Levered her hands from her face.

'Now look at me, girl!'

'Jimmy!'

She clung to him. He felt the wet soaking his shirt.

'Jimmy!'

'All right. All right, girl. Everything will be all right.'

'They want to take me away. Nick does. To London. He's going to give me some injections.'

'He won't hurt you. Just little pinpricks.'

'I don't want to go. Jimmy, I don't want to go.'

'I know. But you're going.'

She tried to pull away. He held her.

'No.'

'Yes, you are.'

'No. Nick can't do that.'

Jimmy shook her.

'Do you want those blinking things in your head for the rest of your life?' His fingers dug into her arms. 'Do you? Do you want to go round blowing things up?

157

Killing people? Do you know what's in your head? Do you?'

Her face was white.

'Things,' Jimmy said. 'Little cells. They live on starlight which you feed them. They passed from the rabbit into you when it bit you. They're inside you now, little cells. OK. So it's tough on them. Hard luck. Nick's going to give you antibiotics and kill them, but it's got to be done. You can't keep them, Jane. You've kept them long enough.'

She was staring at him, grey eyes, staring horrified eyes. That's it, girl. You stare. It's wrong to destroy life. You said it. I heard you. You said it or they did. You won't destroy me.

'Give it, Jane. Come on. Hate me. You can't blow me up, girl. You can pour all the power you like into me. Send it all out. I won't explode. I'm human, not a machine. That's it. Let it come. All the power you've got.'

It came invisibly, through him, round him, spinning through the trees up to the sky where it came from. In Jane's eyes he saw tiredness replace fear.

'Now,' Jimmy said. 'Now girl, I can talk to you. I can talk to *you* and *you* can listen. They've got nothing left to give you. They've got no power. Nick can take them away. You've got to go with him and let him take them away. Jane? Are you listening?'

'Yes.'

'Are you coming home, Jane?'

She was shaking, cold in the early morning sun. Jimmy rubbed her arms. She caught her lip with her teeth to stop it trembling. Jimmy saw a trickle of blood.

'Are you coming home, girl?' She nodded.

Jimmy smiled and squeezed her hand. She glanced down. Jimmy was holding her hand. She bent her head, lifted his hand and sank her teeth into his wrist. The blood from her lip merged with Jimmy's blood, tasting sweet. Jimmy gasped as she pulled her mouth away. Tiny particles like rainbow smoke danced for a moment in the sun and were gone.

Jimmy recoiled and fell against the wall.

'No!'

Jane stood up and backed away. What had she done to Jimmy? What had she done to put horror on his face?

'No!'

It was a choked whisper. One drop of Jimmy's blood fell on a stone. Jane whirled and ran, away from the sunrise, into the woods and the last scent of bluebells. Alan was going down the path. She didn't feel alone any more.

Jimmy stared at his bleeding wrist, then wrapped a handkerchief round it. On the dark far horizon, above the stark cliffs of Elgin and Winnard's Leap the stars were still shining, huge and golden and silent, pouring down their power.